WESTERN BRIDE

Copper Kings - Book 1

JANELLE DANIELS

Dream Cache Publishing

Abby Winthrop knows what life-altering love is like—and how it can destroy you. Now, all her dreams hang on the new women arriving in Promise Creek, hoping they'll become like sisters to her. But when Lucas McDermott, the man who abandoned her years before, turns out to be one of the notorious Copper Kings and is charged with settling the new women, Abby's life is thrown into chaos.

Lucas McDermott is a man of action. When he and his partners strike the richest copper mine in the world, he won't let anything stop their success—especially not a woman from his past. But when he lays eyes on Abby again, plans change. She isn't just a woman he once desired, but the only woman who has ever touched his heart.

Determined to win her back, he proposes a friendship between them. But when Abby is attacked, his protective instincts rise. He loves her still, but can Abby forgive him for past mistakes...or will history repeat itself?

Abby Winthrop knows what life-altering love is like—and how it can destroy you. Now, all her dreams hang on the new women arriving in Promise Creek, hoping they'll become like sisters to her. But when Lucas McDermott, the man who abandoned her years before, turns out to be one of the notorious Copper Kings and is charged with settling the new women, Abby's life is thrown into chaos.

Lucas McDermott is a man of action. When he and his partners strike the richest copper mine in the world, he won't let anything stop their success—especially not a woman from his past. But when he lays eyes on Abby again, plans change. She isn't just a woman he once desired, but the only woman who has ever touched his heart.

Determined to win her back, he proposes a friendship between them. But when Abby is attacked, his protective instincts rise. He loves her still, but can Abby forgive him for past mistakes...or will history repeat itself?

To sign up for Janelle Daniels' readers club and receive notice of new titles as they are available, go to
www.janelledaniels.com

CHAPTER 1

Once a person's heart breaks, it never truly heals. But with time, like any other part of the body, it mends, gets stronger, and figures out how to go on.

At age twenty-six, Abby Winthrop was familiar with that process. Her heart was whole, but it had been sewn together with large, uneven stitches that the most inept seamstress would cringe at.

In fact, that was the whole reason she found herself standing on the platform in Promise Creek, waiting for the train she spied in the distance. Without a broken heart, she would've never traveled here a year ago.

She shifted her heavy basket to the opposite hand. The food inside, prepared by her lovely cook and housekeeper, Sylvia, seemed to get heavier by the minute. But Abby didn't mind.

After several day's travel, she was sure the ladies she waited for would be ravenous. She'd also packed enough for the Copper King who was meeting them here, but since he was one of the wealthiest people in the country, she was sure such offerings were beneath him.

The name was fitting, she mused. A group of six men had claimed a copper mine not far from here, one larger than anyone had ever seen. That alone would make them kings, but they were also tycoons from the East. At least, that's what everyone said. She didn't know who the men were, but wondered if she'd known them in her past life as one of society's darlings, an heiress worth millions. She was sure her brother, Rhys, would. With one of the largest hotel empires in the country, Rhys knew everyone.

As the train moved closer, its steam rising in the air, nervous energy filled her. She'd arrived in Promise Creek a little over a year ago, alone, out of money, and with nowhere to go. If it hadn't been for Ivan's brides who'd taken over his estate after he died, Abby would've been living on the streets. Only one of them was still living in the house when she'd arrived, so they allowed Abby to stay in the sprawling home indefinitely. Besides Sylvia, she'd lived alone for the past year after Willow, the last remaining of Ivan's brides, had married Rhys.

But today, that would all change.

She just wished she wasn't so nervous. If the women didn't like her, there was nothing she could do about it. But Ivan's brides had shown her what true sisterhood was like, and she craved that for herself.

So no matter who these women were, no matter where they came from, Abby was determined to welcome them with open arms. Everyone deserved a chance, and if these women were coming *here*, it was likely their last chance.

The porter, an older gentleman, called out a greeting to her, and she acknowledged him with a smile and a small wave. Things were so different here compared to how she'd grown up in Manhattan, and she loved it. Every single second of it. Here, everyone knew her name, and she knew theirs. It was the charm of living in a small town.

Manhattan had suited her as a young girl—its wealth, high society, glitter, and glamour—but things changed. *People* changed. When she'd left New York, Abigail—the demure, wealthy, responsible woman—had stayed. And here in Promise Creek, Abby was born. Here, she had the freedom to do as she pleased. She wouldn't be forced to marry someone she didn't love, and she didn't answer to anyone—*especially* not society.

These women would be no different. They were coming here for a new start, a change, and she was determined to help them every step of the way.

The train pulled into the station, and a loud, drawn-out whistle announced its arrival. Her stomach flipped, and she placed a hand over it. *Settle down.* She didn't want the women to think she was a ninny.

She took a deep breath and blew it out slowly as people disembarked from the train.

Maybe I should've brought Rhys. She cut off any other thoughts of her brother. She loved him and appreciated everything he'd done for her, how he protected her and looked after her, but she could do this on her own. He'd been there for her when Lucas had broken her heart and left her all those years ago. No matter how many times she'd told him she had enough money for the both of them, it hadn't been enough. *She* hadn't been enough. It was time to stand on her own two feet.

She let out a frustrated huff. If she really needed to wallow in the past, she could do so in the privacy of her own room. Right now, she had a job to do. She schooled her face into a mask of serenity, one that was second nature after years of being forced to wear it. She didn't don it often, out west, but in this case, it was necessary. She needed to act the part of the sophisticated lady. This Copper King was sure to expect it from her, and she wouldn't do anything that would reflect poorly on Rhys or her widowed mother. One whiff that Abby had turned savage in the West, and her mother would be a laughingstock.

With any luck, the man would be someone she'd never met, and she'd only need speak with him briefly before fixing all her attention on the women. And even if they were acquainted, what would it matter? The Copper Kings knew she was living in the house they had rented for the ladies they were bringing in to help settle the town, so it wouldn't be a surprise.

Large groups of single men, a few families, and men escorting their wives filtered out of the train cars. But after a moment, her eyes fell on a woman with fiery red hair tumbling over her shoulders in long, loose curls. The woman scanned the platform as if memorizing every inch of it, then nodded minutely in satisfaction. Abby would have missed it if she hadn't been staring at the porcelain-fine features of her face.

Abby waved, catching her attention, and the woman walked over. There was a light dusting of freckles over the bridge of her nose, which Abby found charming as the woman smiled warmly.

"Are you one of the other ladies who've been brought here?" the woman asked.

"No, but we'll be staying together for the near future. I thought I would meet you here to greet you. I'm Abby Winthrop."

"Lily Reed." She held out her hand, and Abby took the firm grip. "It's so nice to meet you. I'm glad I'm finally here."

Abby grinned. "I'm thrilled you are too. I've been living alone in the house for a year. Well, me and Sylvia."

"Sylvia?"

"She's both the housekeeper and cook. She lives in a small cottage near the house."

Lily seemed taken aback, some of her no-nonsense facade evaporating. "We'll have someone taking care of the house and cooking for us?"

Abby smiled slowly. "Yes. Is that all right?"

Lily nodded slowly. "Yes. I just..." She made a small sound of frustration. "Oh, bother. I've never had help. I'm so used to cleaning and cooking and laundry I'm not sure what I'll do with myself."

"I'm sure you won't be alone there. Several of the women who lived in the house before me were the same. It'll be an adjustment, but I hope it'll be a pleasant one."

Lily grinned. "Oh, I shall enjoy it immensely."

"Excellent." Abby's gaze was drawn to another woman who was already making her way toward them. Her blonde hair, all tightly spiraled curls, bounced with each step.

When she made it to them, her cornflower-blue eyes sparkled with delight. "Since you're the only two single women on the platform, I'm assuming this is where I should be."

Abby nodded. "Were you brought here for work?"

"Yes! It's so exciting." she said teasingly. "I'm Charlotte Hayer."

"Abby Winthrop, and this is Lily Reed."

"Nice to meet you both." Charlotte turned her attention back to the train. "I wonder how many others there are."

"There should be three more."

Charlotte gestured to the end of the platform, where a brunette and a woman with honey-blonde hair waited. "They're probably with us."

Lily waved but got no response. "I don't think they've seen us yet."

"Why don't we go to them?" Abby offered.

In silent agreement, the three set off. When they approached the two women, the blonde looked relieved.

"Thank heavens! I ran into Emery on the train"—she notched her head toward the dark-haired woman—"but I wasn't sure where to go from here."

Emery smiled ruefully. "I told you we would have found our way regardless. I'm sure I could've gotten directions in town."

The other woman rolled her eyes playfully. "At least now, we don't have to hunt anyone down. I'm Grace Cooper, by the way." She nodded to the group in greeting.

Emery did the same. "Emery Kane."

Abby and the other two introduced themselves. "I guess that leaves just one more woman and the Copper King."

Emery raised a dark brow. "Copper King?"

"The men who brought you here," Abby explained. "They're called the Copper Kings because their claim is a massive copper mine. And they're supposedly tycoons from the East."

"Ah." Emery didn't seem too impressed by the information, which only made Abby like her more. Too many people were dazzled by wealth.

A couple stepped off the train, but Abby knew the gorgeous-looking woman wasn't one of them. She'd only taken a glance at the man's expensive, tailored suit and his physique which filled it out perfectly, before looking over at the woman. Her light-brown hair was perfectly coiffed, and her tasteful attire appeared unwrinkled after the long trip. Abby had no idea how she'd managed such a thing. She herself had looked like a rumpled mess when she'd finally gotten to Promise Creek.

Maybe she should ask the woman for traveling tips. The thought made her chuckle. Abby turned to say something to the others when a voice interrupted.

"Looks like we're all here," a man said next to her. The

hairs on Abby's arms rose. "I hope you all had a pleasant journey."

The women around her straightened as the man spoke, giving him their full attention, but Abby couldn't catch her breath enough to look up at his face. Her eyes focused on his polished, expensive shoes and the dark blue suit pants cut from luxurious material.

"Miss Winthrop," he said in greeting.

Her gut clenched, and she closed her eyes, praying for strength. She knew that voice. Years ago it had whispered hotly in her ear, words of love and dreams of the future, and it had haunted her for the eight years since.

Finally, she looked up and met his eyes. Brown, piercing, gorgeous eyes she'd looked into hundreds of times in the past. Eyes she thought she'd never see again. "Mr. McDermott." She couldn't choke out anything else.

Lucas was here.

A heady rush wove through her as he looked over her before giving his attention back to the other women—like seeing her again wasn't shattering. She thought she might faint or vomit or run screaming and crying, but fortunately, she did none of those things.

She locked her knees, praying to keep herself upright as conversation flowed around her. She briefly heard Lucas introduce the pristine woman who accompanied him as Hannah Pierce. Apparently, they'd been seated in the more luxurious portion of the train together. Other than that, Abby couldn't follow the flow of conversation, couldn't understand what anyone was saying. It was like standing in the middle of a thousand beehives.

"Miss Winthrop?" The question sounded far away. "Miss Winthrop?"

The words jarred her back. "Sorry." She looked around the group, having no idea who'd spoken. "Yes?"

Lily looked worriedly between Abby and Lucas. "I asked where I should direct the porter with our trunks."

"Oh, um. I brought a wagon to transport your belongings and extra horses to ride back to the house. I also packed sandwiches if you're hungry." She lamely held the basket up in front of her. "Or we could eat at the hotel, if you'd like to rest before continuing on."

Before the topic could be debated, Lucas said, "We should continue to the house. There is still much to do, and we want to arrive before dark."

The others agreed with him, but Abby wondered if he knew Rhys owned the hotel and only wanted to avoid him while in the presence of the other women. He couldn't avoid him altogether though. There weren't many options for lodging.

She closed her eyes, just barely stifling a groan. Her brother would be apoplectic seeing Lucas again.

But closing her eyes had been a mistake. With Lucas so close, his scent wrapped around her, caressing her like it had so often in the past. The spiced, woodsy scent mingled with his skin, giving off an aroma which made her mouth water. She knew if she tucked her head into his neck, it would be even stronger. She shivered as memories abraded her.

The women looked to her, and the smile she gave them only wavered once—a huge accomplishment, in her opinion. "Let me speak with the porter, and we'll be on our way."

She wished she felt as confident as she sounded, but with Lucas here, there was little chance of that.

CHAPTER 2

Lucas glanced over from his horse, eyeing the way Abigail handled the reins of the wagon. She was poised, confident, and as beautiful as he remembered—maybe even more so. The young girl he'd imagined himself in love with years ago had matured into a woman men would die for.

Seeing her on the platform had jolted him. He'd expected to ride out to the house with the women, give Abigail a polite greeting, and then be on his way. He was here for business, to secure the women in the house and fulfill his other responsibilities. He had no time for distractions, and he'd assured his partners nothing would keep him from doing what needed to be done. And he was surprised to realize Abigail *was* a distraction.

Over the years, he'd convinced himself that what he'd felt for her had been a passing fancy. He'd been low and poor, and she'd been like a sweet in a candy shop. Anyone would want her. It had been best to leave her and make something of himself. And even though he knew he'd broken her heart, it had ultimately been for her good. Had he stayed, they would have both been ruined. Her father had been vicious, and if

Lucas had run away with his daughter, he would have disinherited her without blinking. Lucas hadn't been willing to put her in that situation.

He'd been sure his feelings were in the past, but seeing her now tugged at something in his heart. *I'm just curious about her.* Even as he tried to convince himself of it, it didn't entirely ring true.

Abigail chatted with Charlotte, Grace, and occasionally Hannah, when the woman deigned to speak, but she'd offered no overtures to him. In fact, she acted as though he wasn't there at all.

If it wasn't for her reaction when he'd first spoken, he would wonder if she remembered him at all. She was incredibly beautiful, wealthy, and he knew for a fact she was brilliant and would make a wonderful wife for any man. Why she was in Promise Creek at all was a mystery.

Abigail pointed to the curve in the road. "Just around there, we'll see the house."

The rest of the women perked up, curious about the place they'd call home for the near future. He was also intrigued. Abigail had lived in a palace in Manhattan. Nothing out here could possibly compare.

He rode ahead of the wagon and stopped once the house came into view. It wasn't grand by New York standards, but the sprawling two-story home was much larger than he'd anticipated. It seemed almost ridiculous a house this size had been built so far outside of town. Oh, he'd heard the stories about the man who'd built it. People called him Crazy Ivan, and Lucas agreed with the moniker. What kind of person build a house like this and ordered ten mail-order brides?

One woman was more than enough. Especially the right one.

He cursed as he instinctively glanced at Abigail. She wasn't the right one, and she never had been. They'd been young, their love juvenile. And he was arrogant and cocky to think seeing Abigail wouldn't affect him.

His attention was drawn as all the women—except Hannah, of course—squealed in delight when they saw their new home. Hannah, though, had a curve on her lips, so he knew she must be pleased. He hadn't spent much time with her, but she was the typical woman he'd gotten to know since building his fortune. Proper, elegant, charming. But her charm seemed manufactured, nothing like the cheerful, innocent allure Abigail possessed.

As they pulled in front of the house, Abigail secured the reins and swung down from her perch before he could assist her. She hadn't even glanced in his direction. Most of the women followed suit, but Hannah and Charlotte accepted his aid.

Abigail turned to the women, gesturing widely. "Welcome home! I hope you'll love it here as much as I do. Don't worry about the horses, Sylvia, our housekeeper will see to them. And believe me, you'll hear about it if you do something she deems to be in her domain.'"

The front door opened behind Abigail, and a handsome, older woman with silver-streaked hair and soft features stepped out. "You better heed Abby's warning, or you'll be sorry," the woman said.

When she smiled warmly, fine wrinkles raced over her smooth-looking skin. "I'm Sylvia. I wanted to quickly welcome you all. If there's anything you need, please ask. I know how hard it is to move somewhere new. And no matter how different this place may be, if you keep an open mind, you'll come to love it here too."

Lucas glanced at Abigail, surprised the housekeeper had addressed her as Abby. She'd never gone by anything other than Abigail, and it took him aback. What else had changed? He glanced over her form while she chatted with the women, and a surge of desire swept through him. Her body had filled out in every place a man fancied. She was a goddess.

Her clothes appeared to be of the finest quality, so he guessed she was still as wealthy as ever. It only made him wonder again why she was here.

When there was a lull, Lucas stepped toward the group. "Why don't you go in and have Sylvia and Miss Winthrop show you to your rooms? I'll take care of the trunks."

Sylvia frowned. "That isn't necessary, sir. I can manage."

He gave her a nod. "I imagine you can, but I would like to do it, if that's all right."

Sylvia seemed surprised. Finally, she nodded and gave him a warm smile. "All right."

He was turning toward the trunks when he noticed Abigail watching him, a frown on her face. But, before he could say anything, she ripped her gaze from him and followed the others into the house.

Laughter echoed out the front door, and a small smile crossed his lips as he hefted the first trunk from the wagon. The women seemed pleased with the place, and that was one thing he'd aimed to accomplish. He wanted them settled and happy. They'd have plenty of time to get comfortable in their new home before he placed them elsewhere. He wasn't completely sure where yet, but he figured it would come to him.

He brought the trunk inside and heard chatter on the second floor. With only four bedrooms, two of the rooms would need to be shared. He imagined Abigail would keep her own room since she was a permanent resident here.

He looked around at the grand, two-story entrance, the plush sitting room off the foyer, the expensive decor and knickknacks gracing the tables—all sitting behind a door with a lock he could pick in ten seconds.

He frowned and knelt, inspecting the door's hardware.

Had Rhys truly allowed his sister to live here with so little protection? It was mind blowing. Anyone could have broken in, stolen from her—or worse—stolen *her*.

How had she survived an entire year here?

"Is something wrong?"

Lucas glanced over his shoulder, forcing his body to react slowly, naturally. It was hard. Abigail's smoky, tantalizing voice caused all sorts of physical responses in him. He looked back at the lock. "Yes. This is insufficient. You're in here like a fresh loaf of bread while starving men circle the bakery."

There was a moment of silence before her laughter echoed from the top of the stairs.

He froze. Of all the reactions he'd expected, that wasn't one of them. He glanced over his shoulder with a raised brow.

She shook her head chidingly. "Oh, Mr. McDermott, come now. I'm practically a spinster. I'm perfectly safe here." Another chuckle escaped. "But thank you for amusing me."

He didn't know why, but having her address him so formally chaffed. "You used to call me Lucas."

Her spine straightened, and the smile fell from her lips. "That was a long time ago." She tipped her head. "Excuse me."

She descended the stairs and walked down another hall. She wasn't quite running, but her pace had quickened as if she couldn't get away from him fast enough. Before he realized what he was doing, he followed her.

ABBY BURST THROUGH THE BACK DOOR, HER LUNGS burning for air. She needed a moment. Just one single moment to get herself back under control.

She strode to the copse of trees not far from the house. She wasn't running away from Lucas. This was an act of self-preservation. When he'd walked out of her life all those years ago, she'd been devastated. Well, he wasn't going to crush her now.

She blew out a shallow breath, calming her heart. This was *her* life, and Lucas, *Mr. McDermott*, had no place in it. So, she wasn't running away from him. She just didn't want anything to do with him, didn't even want to see him—no matter how handsome he was.

Stop it!

She needed to stop thinking of him. He was here to do a job, and she needed to help the women find their place here. This was her life. This was her future. And Lucas didn't have a part in either.

She sucked in a few deep breaths, pressing her hand against her corseted stomach. *I can do this. I can do this.* She opened her eyes and nodded. She *could* do this. She was strong. She was capable. Treating Lucas as an acquaintance only was something she could manage.

He probably thought she was ridiculous for leaving as she had just now, but she didn't care. It didn't matter what he thought. She was her own woman, and it would be good for him to see that.

Determined, she whipped around, ready to march back into the house—and ran into a wall. Someone grunted, and she realized it wasn't a wall, but a man. His arms wrapped around her as she teetered, and she gasped. She fought off a shiver as Lucas' delicious scent assailed her.

"Steady," he cautioned, keeping his arms around her. "You ran into me pretty hard. You aren't injured, are you?"

His minty breath wafted through her hair, and he ran his hands up and down her arms, searching for injuries. She flashed back to all those years ago when they were together, holding each other like this, and pain slashed through her.

She brought her hands up between them and pushed,

every inch of his chest as sculpted as when he'd lived a life of hard labor. Couldn't he have at least softened? Become just a little less appealing?

She stepped back from him, clearing her throat. "Pardon. I didn't see you there."

"I can see that. Forgive me for intruding."

All this formality was becoming unbearable. "Is there something you need, Mr. McDermott?" She still refused to call him Lucas. Lucas was the man she'd loved, the man she'd thought she'd spend the rest of her life with. And that man no longer existed.

"I wanted to speak with you."

"About?"

He watched her for a moment. She raised an eyebrow, and he looked away, cursing softly under his breath before raking a hand through his hair. "Look, I know this is complicated, but I want to make this work."

"It's not complicated at all. You're here to do a job—to get these women settled and start things at the mine." She let out a breath. "There is nothing between us, and frankly, nothing else needs to be said. You'll go your way, and I'll go mine."

He shifted uneasily as if uncertain whether to believe her or not. She was surprised she'd sounded so confident.

"Simple as that, huh?"

"Simple as that." She held out her hands like it could truly be that easy. "There needn't be anything more."

"I'll need to come by often for the first while to talk with the women about their long term arrangements as they're worked out."

"You're welcome to do so. I'll stay out of your way."

"You don't need to do that."

There was an edge to his voice now. She was getting to him, and she couldn't help but needle further. It wasn't right, but she couldn't stop a little of her hurt from eking out and stabbing him. "Of course," she demurred, knowing he would hate it. There wasn't a demure bone in her body, and they both knew it.

His jaw clenched, but she kept up her innocent expression. After a few moments, she asked, "Is there something else I can help you with?"

"No. I just wanted to come to an understanding."

"We have." Her tone was flat.

He finally nodded and started to head back to the house, but she could tell he wasn't happy.

"Oh, Mr. McDermott?" Catching his attention, he turned back to her. "While I might have no trouble interacting with you in the future, I'm afraid my brother won't take kindly to you being here. I'm sure you're aware he owns the only hotel in town."

He nodded grimly. "I'm aware. I'll figure a way around him."

Her first true smile since seeing him lifted her lips. "For your sake, I hope so."

CHAPTER 3

Lucas casually walked into the hotel in Promise Creek. He didn't know what he'd been expecting, but this wasn't it. The other Winthrop hotels he'd stayed in had been cool, polished, and possessed a layer of elegance only the wealthy could afford. The decor and design of their hotels changed with each location, echoing the local community, but it was always clear they were part of the Winthrop empire.

This hotel, while still possessing the polish he'd expected, was unlike any other. The entrance was smaller, cozier. He felt more intrigued by the décor than dazzled, and as he walked farther into the marbled and heavily-paneled lobby, he realized he also felt comfortable.

Even after making his first few millions, whenever he stepped into opulent structures, a part of him feared he still wasn't good enough. That he never would be. He didn't feel like that here, and he paused for a moment to figure out why. What was it about the place that welcomed him instead of intimidated him?

A woman with golden-blonde hair stepped toward him, a

friendly smile on her face. "Welcome to the Promise Creek Hotel."

Lucas offered the woman a warm smile and a polite bow in greeting before he took in the expensive cut and materials of her gown. Whoever this woman was, she was wealthy. She wasn't just a greeter for the establishment. "It's a pleasure to be here."

"You're most welcome. Are you here for a meal or a room?"

"Both." He took a deep breath and gave her an honest, appreciative smile. "And from the look and smell of it, I've come to the right place."

Her lips quirked. "You have. Are you planning to stay long?" she asked, her curiosity evident.

"I am, if everything goes according to plan."

She beamed. "Excellent. Let me lead you to the front desk and they'll help you get checked in, Mr...?" She blushed. "Forgive me. I forgot introductions. I'm Willow Winthrop, and you are?"

He glanced over the woman again, taking in every inch of her appearance. So, this was who Rhys had married. She was warm and friendly and genuine, and it surprised him. He'd always thought the Winthrop heir would choose a cold, blue-blooded kind of woman.

He also knew she was one of the owners of the house they were renting. He held out his hand, guessing she would appreciate the gesture. "I'm Lucas McDermott." He paused, expecting a reaction, but didn't get one. Interesting. Maybe Rhys and Abigail had never mentioned him. "I'm one of the owners of the new copper mine."

She squeaked. "One of the Copper Kings?" She closed her eyes tight and sealed her mouth, as if berating herself for the slip. "Forgive me. That's what everyone is calling you around here."

He smiled, amused. "No apologies necessary. Every man wants to be a king."

Her eyes crinkled as she laughed. "Indeed. Well, from all I hear, you are definitely that."

He had no qualms about discussing money. Unlike so many in the upper crust, he was proud of what he'd earned and what he'd done to get it. "Thank you, but I must admit I'm one of the smaller partners."

"Hmm." She looked like she didn't believe him, but he didn't argue the point further. "Well, we are glad to have you. Would you like a tray sent to your room, or would you prefer the dining room? I can have either arranged for you."

"Please don't trouble yourself, Mrs. Winthrop. I'll make my way to the dining room when I'm settled."

"Nonsense. And you might as well call me Willow. You'll be here for some time, and we *are* doing business together outside of your stay here. I'll have a table waiting for you whenever you're ready."

He was humbled by her generosity. "Thank you."

"It's my pleasure. We're grateful to—"

She broke off when Rhys wrapped possessive arms around her and pulled her in tight. The glare he sent Lucas was ominous, and he could guess what Rhys held back behind the glowering stare.

Lucas waited, calculating what Rhys would do next. It was something he excelled at. Waiting, watching—then making his move.

He could see Rhys' thoughts clearly. He wanted to throw him out...but would he?

Willow seemed to sense something was off, and paused to look between the two of them. "Is there something I should know?" she finally asked, as she worried her lip with her teeth.

Lucas smiled at her, and Rhys growled. "Don't look at her."

"Rhys!" Willow yelled, shocked at his behavior.

Rhys gently squeezed her, and Lucas was amused when, instead of quieting down, Willow turned on him. "Tell me what is going on! This is Mr. McDermott. He's one of the copper mine owners."

Rhys looked up from his wife, his eyes narrowing. "Oh, is he?"

"I am," Lucas said confidently. "I've already settled the women at the house."

"You what?" Rhys' question was spoken softly, deadly. "You went to the house? Was Abby there?"

Willow looked even more concerned now. Before Lucas could answer, she placed her hand on Rhys' chest. "Perhaps this conversation is better had in the office."

Rhys' jaw clenched, but he finally nodded. "Follow me." He still held Willow's hand as he turned toward the back hallway. Willow sent Lucas a sympathetic smile, obviously knowing he'd done something to infuriate her husband.

They walked down tidily kept halls where only the servants trespassed, but as he'd expected, the corridors were well maintained with floor polish and freshly painted walls. He didn't spy even one scuff mark on the trim. Winthrop could pocket more if he didn't hold to such rigid maintenance standards in non-public areas, but if this were Lucas' business, he'd do the same.

Rhys opened an unassuming door and ushered Willow in, leaving Lucas to follow them. As expected, Rhys took command of the situation from behind the desk and didn't offer Lucas a seat. "So, you're here for the copper mine."

"Yes. I'm sure you've acquired as much information as possible about the operation."

"I have, and I was fine with it, happy even—until now.

Why wasn't I told of your involvement when Mr. Eversly came to us a few weeks ago?"

Lucas wasn't going to pull any punches. "I'm sure you can guess why."

Rhys' nostrils flared. "You deliberately misled us? What else have you and the other *Copper Kings* lied about?"

"We lied about nothing." It took everything Lucas had to keep a level voice. He was always cool in moments like these. It was what had helped him succeed. But the one thing he couldn't tolerate was being called a liar. "Mr. Eversly omitted my involvement for obvious reasons, but nothing more."

Willow cleared her throat. "While I'm sure those reasons are quite clear to Rhys, I'm afraid I have no idea what is going on."

Lucas expected Rhys to tell his wife to be quiet, but instead, he gave her his full attention. "Has Abby ever mentioned her past?"

"No..." She drew out the word as she glanced at Lucas. "But I'm assuming Mr. McDermott is involved in it?"

"Yes." Rhys glared at Lucas again. "She'd formed an attachment to him, and then he left her. Her heart was broken."

Lucas had known Abby would be hurt when he left, but he'd done it for her own good. He wasn't going to bring her down to his level, to thrust her into a world where she didn't belong. He'd loved her too much for that. Besides, she'd recovered just as he knew she would. A little hurt when he left was better than a lifetime of pain and regrets.

Willow narrowed her eyes at him. "I see." Obviously, she was close with her sister-in-law.

Rhys nodded roughly then placed both his palms flat on the desk and leaned forward, eyeing Lucas. "We have a problem. The lease on the house is locked down tight, thanks to your lawyers, and there's no getting out of it. Also, the claim is already yours, and I know no matter how much I fight it, I'll never win. But then, I'm sure you arranged it all that way."

Lucas inclined his head. "If our situations were reversed, I doubt you'd do anything differently."

He could see Rhys wanted to disagree, but Lucas knew one thing about the man—he was honorable to a fault and never condoned lying. It was something they had in common.

"Just tell me. Are you staying long?" Rhys asked.

"Yes. Several months, at least."

Rhys looked away and swore quietly. "You've put me in a bad position, Lucas."

Lucas nodded, acknowledging it easily. He'd known both Abigail and Rhys lived in the area, but he truly thought everything between them would have been long forgotten. It had almost been eight years since he'd left her. She didn't still have feelings for him. He would have sensed them when he'd spoken to her at the house. No, this was Rhys being overprotective of her, as he'd always been.

Rhys finally hung his head. "There's nothing I can do here, no matter how much I want to." He looked up at Lucas and pinned him. "Just stay away from her. That much I can demand."

Lucas raised a brow. "Are you in a position to demand anything from me?"

His words brought a faint smile to Rhys' face. "If you want a place to sleep that doesn't involve a tent and a cot, then yes."

It was Lucas who wanted to smile now. Time to negotiate. "I'll stay away from her as well as I can, but I still have to do my job, which will require me to visit the house."

"Then other than pleasantries, don't speak to her. Don't even look at her."

Lucas rocked back on his heels. "Would you have me ignore her if she decides to speak with me?"

"No." He growled. "But you'll not hurt her again."

"Then that's simple," he said, as if no other discussion were necessary. "Abigail will remain unharmed during my stay."

"Abby," Willow said, interrupting the conversation. "She goes by Abby now."

"Miss Winthrop," Rhys corrected, his voice a growl.

Lucas nodded in easy agreement. "Miss Winthrop it is. Is there anything else you'd like to discuss?"

The smooth question got under Rhys' skin, if the blotches rising above his collar were any indication. "No. Just stay away from her."

"I intend to." Lucas nodded again before heading out the door. That had been easier than expected. And for some reason, it only made Lucas want to see Abigail again.

CHAPTER 4

"You're going to love it in town," Abby said for what felt like the hundredth time. She held the reins loose as she allowed the wagon's horses to navigate the path to town. "It has almost everything we need, but I'm not going to lie, I'm grateful you're all here. I can't wait to see how you'll change the town once you're placed in positions."

She smiled back at the group of women in the wagon. They'd been so tired from traveling yesterday that they'd hardly spoken, so she didn't know them well. But the things she could discern intrigued her. They all appeared to be of very different backgrounds and temperament.

"Is there anything in particular you each wish to do?" she asked, hoping to start a conversation. "Anyone want to be a teacher?" She chuckled. "The town desperately needs one. Especially now with the new mine."

The red-headed woman, Lily, spoke up first. "Unfortunately, I don't think teaching would agree with me. I'm not certain what I'd like to do, but definitely not that."

Charlotte, the woman with pale-blond, curly hair, cut in. "Don't you like children?"

"I do, yes. Very much. Just not that many at once."

All the women in the cart laughed. Even Hannah, the pristine-looking goddess, chuckled. She was a lot like the women Abby had known back east, but Abby was determined to give her a fair shot, just like the others. "What about you, Hannah? Anything you'd like to do?"

She smiled, and, while friendly, Abby could tell her smile was contrived. But she wasn't sure if Hannah was doing it on purpose or if she'd been so long in high society that it was second nature. It had taken some time for Abby herself to adjust to life here. She'd been so lucky to have Willow to help guide her through it. Now it was her turn to do the same.

"I'm afraid I'm rather like Lily. I don't know exactly what I'd like to do in the short term, but long term, I'd like to marry well."

Emery snorted and shook her head, her loose, dark brown curls bouncing around her.

Hannah sat up straight. "I beg your pardon? Is there something you find humorous, Miss Kane?"

Emery wasn't cowed. She looked Hannah directly in the eye. "Yes, actually. I was thinking how completely useless that sounded."

"You think marriage is useless?" Hannah asked smoothly. She appeared regal, serene even, but Abby knew the woman had to be upset.

Emery shrugged. "Not at all. I think marriage and having children is one of the most noble things a woman can do. I certainly hope to find someone to settle down with, but I have other plans as well. I don't exist just to marry—especially for money."

Grace, who sat next to Emery, clucked. "That's unkind. I know we're all different, but we should try to get along. For now, we're living together, and the town is so small we'll likely see each other often. We should at least try."

Emery's brows knitted, but she finally nodded, bowing to Grace's logic. "You're right. I apologize for my rudeness, Hannah. It's not my place to pass judgment on your choices. I hope you're very successful in whatever you pursue."

Hannah smiled, not ruffled at all. "Thank you, Emery. You're very kind."

Ice. That's what Abby thought of when she looked at Hannah.

Emery just looked away and remained silent.

Well this is going well. "Grace, what about you?"

She twirled a strand of her honey-gold hair. "Truthfully, I'd love to have my own claim, but I don't think it's meant to be."

Abby thought about what Willow had told her of their gold mine, especially how much they'd failed when they first tried to learn how to mine themselves. Some of those stories...she snorted just thinking about them. "I think some people are suited to the work, and others not." She chuckled. "The women who own the house inherited a gold mine as well. In the beginning, they thought to mine it themselves. But after their first, and only, disastrous lesson, they decided it was best to hire someone for the job."

Grace grinned. "It definitely takes a certain type of person. I do think I'm suited for it, but I doubt it'll happen. I guess I'll see what Mr. McDermott can find for me."

"Speaking of a certain handsome Copper King," Charlotte said, sending a riot of blond corkscrews arcing as she turned back toward Abby. "What happened the other day between you two?"

"What do you mean?" Abby squeaked.

Lily leaned forward. "There's obviously something between you two. You didn't just meet on the train platform yesterday."

"Oh. Well. It's kind of a long story."

"How about you give us the short story now and more

details later?" Hannah prodded. It was the first time she'd seen a crack in the woman's cool façade.

Abby shifted on the wooden seat. "We knew each other a long time ago. Practically a lifetime ago. He worked for my father in a hotel."

Hannah's head cocked to the side. "You said your name was Abby Winthrop? As in *the* Winthrop hotels?"

"Correct."

"Wow! I've seen one before. It really was something," Charlotte practically bounced in her chair. "Those are your hotels?"

"Not mine. My father's—well, now my brother's."

There was a moment of silence as everyone took that in. No doubt, they were shocked. Abby neither looked nor behaved like an heiress. Not any longer. And she refused to ever don that mask again. She belonged to herself and would do as she pleased.

Lily looked at her seriously, and Abby tried to hold still under her lake-blue stare. "How did you end up here?" the woman finally asked, clearly unable to figure her out.

Abby's grip tightened on the reins. This was murky territory, and she wasn't sure she was ready to talk about it. "That's a long story as well. Basically, my family thought it was time to marry, and I disagreed. So, I ran away."

"You did?" Grace's mouth hung open. "That's so brave. I'm not sure I'd have the guts to head out west without knowing I had something to fall back on if I failed. Really, this position we were offered is ideal."

Charlotte and Emery agreed quietly, but Hannah and Lily remained silent. Abby guessed it was because Hannah was here to snag one of the Copper Kings. As for Lily, she seemed to have a backbone of steel. She would have traveled here alone and pushed forward until she succeeded.

Wanting to change the subject, Abby glanced at Emery. "Do you have something you'd like to do?"

"I'm a nurse," she said easily.

"You are?" Hannah asked, astonishment tinging her voice.

"Yes. I came here because I wanted more opportunity. There isn't a hospital in town, but with the growth here, it's only a matter of time. I want to help set it up."

"That's incredible," Abby said. "I'm impressed."

Emery shrugged. "It's something I love. Taking care of others. Helping them get better. I'm not a traditional nurse, by any means. I might be a bit pushy." She grinned. "But I lose very few patients. So, I must be doing something right."

"Heaven forbid I ever get sick," Hannah said under her breath. Abby guessed Emery heard the comment, but she didn't say anything. Thankfully.

Ignoring the tension, Charlotte said, "I think I want to open a bakery."

All heads swiveled toward the spunky woman. "What kind of bakery?" Abby asked.

"The kinds you see in cities. I'll sell bread and offer a small selection of sandwiches or baskets for lunch. But what I really want to make are pastries and treats. Croissants, macaroons, cookies, cakes, pies, everything."

Abby's mouth watered. "I fully intend to visit you often."

"Sweet tooth?" Charlotte grinned.

"Sweet *teeth*. Every. Single. One. Sylvia is a great cook, but she doesn't do many desserts." She let out a wistful sigh.

Hannah's head cocked to the side. "Are we getting close to town?"

"Right around that corner." They could hear some of the hustle and bustle in the distance. "What should we do first?"

A chorus of "eat and shop!" filled the air, and the women laughed. It was the first cohesive moment they'd had. No one

fought. No one argued. They were just women—maybe even friends.

It was everything Abby had hoped for.

A few minutes later, they entered Main Street. They'd passed through there the day before, but they'd been so tired, they hadn't taken in their surroundings. Pretty houses, which were tidy and well kept, lined the end of the street, and Abby knew who lived in each one. It was something she loved about living here. With so few people, everyone knew each other.

"Lovely," Lily said, appreciatively. "It's nice when people have pride in where they live."

Abby hadn't thought of it that way before. "They do," she agreed.

Hannah looked around, frowning. "Are there any larger homes?"

Emery groaned, and Grace poked her, as if telling her to behave. Abby pretended not to notice. "Not in town. Everything is smaller here and clustered, but there are several large estates outside of town. A lot of miners settled down and started ranching after their claims paid out, then built mansions on their land."

"That's what I would do too," Grace said, grinning. "Maybe I'll have to abandon the Copper Kings and make my own way." They all chuckled again.

As they pulled closer to the town square, Abby pointed out several of the buildings and points of interest.

Hannah frowned again. "No library?"

Emery guffawed. "You're asking about a library?"

Hannah's back went rigid. "Do you have a problem with books?"

It was the first time she'd heard an edge in Hannah's voice. Emery had hit a nerve. "Books are wonderful," Abby quickly answered. "Unfortunately, the town doesn't have a library yet. I know several people with large collections though. One of the house's owners, Juliette MacAllister, has a large collection, and one of the neighboring ranch owners, Owen Judd, also has a vast library. He married one of Ivan's brides as well."

"Ivan's brides?" Lily asked.

Now Abby grinned. "Another long story, but the man who built the house was a crazy miner. His claim hadn't paid out, but money trickled in. He decided it was time to get married, so he ordered ten brides."

"Ten?" Hannah asked, scandalized.

Emery shook her head. "Why would he do that?"

"He wanted options."

Grace and Charlotte laughed while the other three groaned.

"This town is so strange," Lily said.

Abby grinned. "You have no idea." She saw an opening in front of the mercantile and maneuvered the wagon in front of it.

The moment the vehicle stopped, she realized her mistake. "Everyone stay in the wagon," she said, as the men converged.

She been so busy chatting that she hadn't been paying attention.

A crowd gathered, and, while they just stood around, smiling, waving, and shouting things to them, she knew things could get out of hand quickly with a group this size.

"What's happening?" Lily finally shouted.

Everyone leaned closer to Abby, so they could hear her over the men. "They're single and want wives! I forgot this could happen. There was a lot of interest when I came to town, but nothing like this." She gestured wildly at the crowd. "It must be because there's so many of us now." She berated herself.

"What do we do?" Grace called out. "We can't get down!"

"Stay in the wagon! Someone will help us."

"Someone will help?" Hannah shook her head. "Who? Anyone who had the inclination would end up joining the group down there."

One of the men reached out and touched Hannah's skirt. She smacked his hand, and the man pulled it back, but didn't look repentant at all. He only grinned and kissed the part of his skin she'd slapped. She stood in the wagon to get the men's attention.

"What are you doing?" Abby hissed. "Don't draw attention to yourself!"

Hannah stopped Abby from pulling her back down, but other than that, she just stood there, looking out at the crowd.

Abby suddenly realized it was getting quieter and quieter —until finally, the men were silent.

Hannah rewarded their behavior with an indulgent smile like she'd give to a pet. "Thank you, gentlemen. Your excitement is a bit overwhelming." She spoke softly, forcing the men to remain quiet so they could hear her. Abby was even amused when several leaned in. Amused—and wary.

"Now," Hannah continued, "we greatly appreciate your welcome, and we look forward to meeting all of you, but we can't possibly do so like this. If you please, back away from the wagon so we can get down."

"Hannah..." Abby didn't like the idea of getting out no matter how tame the men appeared. "I'm not sure this is a good idea."

"They're listening to her," Lily said.

Charlotte looked over the calm crowd. "It looks safe now."

Abby knew nothing could be further from the truth. These men weren't like the ones they knew back east. They were rougher, had less qualms over manners, and they were women-starved. They needed to be careful. Very careful.

As the pack of men slowly moved away from the wagon, Hannah beamed at them. "Thank you. We greatly appreciate it." She lifted the hem of her skirt to climb down, and two men stepped forward, holding out their hands to assist her down.

"Don't," Abby whispered one last time.

"It's all right." Hannah hesitated only a moment before placing her hands in their dirty ones. "They're going to behave now. Aren't you, gentlemen?"

Gentlemen was pushing it. A few were in suits and cleaned up, but the vast majority looked like they'd just come from working a full day in the mines.

"Yes, ma'am, we will," one of the men said. His smile showed a missing tooth.

Everything was going well until that same man tucked Hannah's arm in his own, leaving the second man alone. "Hey. The lady didn't ask to be escorted!"

"Every woman should be escorted. Get one of the other ones."

The man took an aggressive step toward Hannah. "But I want that one."

Hannah yelped as the man who escorted her yanked her closer. "She's with me."

The words were like a flame to dry kindling. Hannah was now held by both men, each yelling their reasons why they should get her. Other men stepped forward to assist, only to get pushed or shouted at.

More men yelled, then chaos erupted as the first punch was thrown.

Abby hopped to the ground and struck one of the men in the arm with the long stick she kept in the wagon. The man whirled around, his arm raised to strike, but instead of cowering, Abby stood her ground, glaring at the man. "Get away from her."

The man gestured to the one still holding onto Hannah. "But he said—"

"Let go of her. Now." Neither moved away, just eying her like they weren't sure what to do. "Now!"

Her yell startled them enough to release Hannah, who quickly moved behind Abby. "Get in the wagon."

Hannah didn't need to be told twice. As she climbed up behind her, Abby didn't turn around. Instead, she faced down the two men who'd assaulted her new friend.

The man who'd held Hannah's arm took a step forward, his face red with indignation. "You had no right to interfere, Miss Winthrop. I was escorting her properly. You should mind your own business."

"Well, as of yesterday, these women *are* my business. And if you haven't already heard, they're protected by the Copper Kings." That seemed to deflate some of the wind in their sails.

At least until the other got his second wind. "Well, they don't own them. They can choose for themselves who courts them."

"That's right," the other man agreed. "Those women are fair game. And so are you." The two men grinned at each other like they'd just had a great idea.

They moved forward slowly, and Abby's stomach dropped. She raised her weapon. "Stay back!"

"Come on now, honey. We won't hurt you. But since you took away the other lady, I think it's only right you spend some time with us."

"I'm not going anywhere with you!" When the first man reached out, she smacked his hand with the stick.

He howled, rubbing the injury before glaring at her. "I like feisty women."

Abby doubted that. He looked furious, and for the first time, Abby was afraid for herself. She glanced around at the crowd, the sounds of grunts and fisticuffs echoing in her ears. No one was paying attention to them. They were too caught up in their own brawls.

The second man moved forward, and she swiped out with her stick, but he sidestepped her swing and caught the end, yanking the weapon from her hand. "I'll take this now."

She held out her hands and screamed, but he grabbed her upper arms and hauled her against him. His nostrils flared as he sensed victory, and his vile breath wafted to her.

"Release me now!"

He just laughed and looked up at the other man. "You're right, Clive. I think I like them feisty too."

Someone in the cart screamed, and she looked up. Other men were reaching into the wagon and grabbing at their skirts. Terror filled her heart. "Let them go! Let them—"

Three gunshots rang in the air.

Everyone stilled, and a moment later, a familiar male voice echoed over the crowd. "Release those women now. You have five seconds until someone gets shot."

CHAPTER 5

Lucas lingered in the hotel lobby, speaking with a gentleman from the East, when he held up his hand, forcing the man to pause mid-sentence. "Do you hear that?" he asked, angling his ear toward the door.

The noise was sporadic, the occasional holler or whistle, but soon, the noise grew louder, more consistent. Lucas' instincts kicked in, and he headed for the hotel door.

The noise grew deafening once he stepped outside. There were men swarming a wagon in front of the mercantile. He cursed, moving forward as a fight broke out and women started yelling. He didn't have to see the women to know they were the ones he'd settled at the house.

He yelled and even threw a few punches of his own, but the men had become a mob. He'd known the difficulties of bring in a group of women to a mining town like this, but he'd had no idea it would be this bad.

He tried again to handle this in a civilized fashion, but as he dodged a punch, he caught sight of pink lace. Lead settled in his gut. One of the women was out of the wagon.

Panicked, he looked up and saw the mob start to pull down the five ladies he'd brought in by train.

That left Abigail. His eyes darted back to where he'd seen the pink through the sea of bodies.

Dread rolled through him, and he started pushing his way through the group, frantic to get to her. A stray punch landed in his stomach, and he bent over, wheezing to catch his breath. His attacker shrugged and went after someone else.

Abigail's scream echoed through the crowd.

Murder spread through his veins. He yanked his gun out of his holster, pointed it to the sky and fired three times.

It had the desired effect.

Sensing danger, the men settled down, wary of Lucas' intentions. "Release the women now. You have five seconds until someone gets shot." He meant it too. If the two men close to Abigail didn't release her and step away immediately, he wouldn't be responsible for his actions.

When neither man moved a muscle, only sizing him up as an opponent, a deadly calm settled over Lucas. He always went numb before a fight. Becoming cold, calculating. But for the first time, a glimmer of rage rose to the surface.

He was angry the women were being attacked, but he was livid that any man dared touch *her*.

He stepped forward, cocking his gun before aiming at one of the men. "Five. Four. Three. Two—" Before he could say one, both men released her and backed away with their hands raised.

Satisfaction wove through him as he quickly glanced at Abigail. She had a small tear in her sleeve, and he swore he would avenge her once they were all safe. Otherwise, she looked unharmed. A little shaken up, but whole.

He directed his weapon at the men surrounding the wagon, still posing a threat to the other ladies. "Move."

They didn't have to be told twice. The men scurried away immediately.

Lucas placed himself between the mob and the wagon. "These women are under my protection. If any of you come near them again, you'll answer to me. Do not touch them, do not approach them, don't even look at them unless they've invited you to do so. Do I make myself clear?"

Several of the men agreed, but there were plenty of grumbles as well. He'd have to deal with that later.

"Good. Now leave." Lucas didn't move from his spot until everyone had left. A few men glared at him as they walked away, and Lucas wondered what kind of trouble they'd bring. He might have to talk to Rhys about it. He hated the necessity, but he had to get information on who he was dealing with. He would do anything to keep Abigail, and the rest of the women, safe.

When he felt the danger pass, he turned to the ladies. "Are you all well? Are any of you injured?"

Lily rubbed her arms. "Only shook up, I think."

He nodded grimly. "I'm sorry for what just happened. I knew you'd receive attention, but I had no idea of the extent."

Abigail's shoulders dropped. "I didn't realize either. I'm sorry. I put you all in jeopardy."

Emery vaulted down from the wagon and placed her hand on Abigail's shoulder. "This isn't your fault. No one could have foreseen this. Never in my wildest dreams would this happen. We'll just have to be more careful next time."

The women started discussing what they should do, but Abigail remained uncharacteristically silent. He moved closer to her. "Are you truly all right?" He reached out to touch her, to pull her in close to him, but realized it was no longer his right.

He curled his fingers into his palms and lowered his hand.

"If you're uncomfortable, I can get Rhys. He can make arrangements for you." It was hard to offer, but she deserved to have someone she loved and respected taking care of her.

She seemed a bit dazed, but finally nodded. "All right. It's probably best he knows about this."

He nodded and then looked at the rest of the women. "Let's go into the hotel and have lunch while we discuss how we're going to avoid this in the future."

The women agreed, and they moved as a unit, each of them sending quick glances over their shoulders to make certain they weren't being followed. They were uneasy, and it boiled his blood that the men in town had scared them. How were they supposed to set up a community, to bring in more women, when the ones they already had were treated harshly?

He glanced over at Abigail, and, while her head was held high, her arms were wrapped around her middle. She was trying to be strong, but he could tell she was struggling. It took every ounce of willpower he had to leave her alone.

They stepped onto the boardwalk, and he ushered the women through the hotel entrance. Instantly, he could tell the women felt safer. Grace, Hannah, and Charlotte lost the look like they were being hunted, and Lily and Emery stopped glanced over their shoulders.

He was about to suggest they move toward the dining room when he met Rhys' furious eyes. Abigail's brother wasted no time in coming over to the group. "What happened? Are you all right?" He stepped closer to his sister, checking to make sure she was sound before leveling a glare at Lucas. "Get away from her."

Lucas didn't blame Rhys in the slightest, but he wasn't about to leave the women alone. His chin notched up as he stood his ground, but before he could stay anything, Abigail reached out and placed a hand on her brother's arm. "It's all right. He saved us, actually."

"Saved you?" Shock and disbelief tinged his voice. "From what?"

Emery explained, "The moment we arrived in town, men swarmed the wagon. They were a little too enthusiastic."

Rhys' jaw clenched, but he nodded, clearly understanding. "But you're well? No one was injured."

"We're fine," Abigail said softly. "They scared us, but if Lucas—*Mr. McDermott*—hadn't been there, it would've been a lot worse."

No one missed her slip, especially Lucas. Hearing her say his name once more filled him with something he'd thought died long before.

Longing.

Unfortunately, Rhys hadn't missed it either. "Thank you for bringing them here," he said through gritted teeth.

"It was the right thing. They need protection."

Rhys nodded, looking over the women. "What's the plan now?" He glanced at his sister. "Are you staying in the hotel?"

Abigail shook her head immediately. "I can't run away from this. It's my life. It's *our* life. We need to return home and move on. The men will calm down, adjust to having more women around. And soon, hopefully, even more will arrive. It'll be all right."

Lucas glanced at Rhys, and their eyes met. They knew such a thing wasn't likely to happen anytime soon.

"We'll figure it out," Rhys said, trying to reassure the group. "Let me get Willow, and we'll meet you in the private dining room. I'll make the arrangements." He'd already signaled his assistant who then gestured for their group to follow him.

Lucas allowed the women to go first, but Abigail remained at the back. He realized she wasn't following. "What is it?" he asked.

She took a deep breath before looking him in the eyes.

The force of those green depths robbed him of breath. She was stunning, gorgeous, and he realized in that moment, he'd never forgotten her. He'd never moved on.

And now, he wasn't sure if he ever would.

"I just wanted to say thank you. For what you did out there. If you hadn't intervened, it would have turned out very differently." She didn't wait for him to respond. Instead, she quickly followed the others, as if scared to hear what he had to say.

She needn't have worried though. He wasn't sure he could even speak. For the first time in eight years, he wondered if leaving had been a mistake.

CHAPTER 6

As everyone filed into the large, private dining room, Abby's muscles unraveled. What had happened with the mob was horrible, but no one could've foreseen it. How were they going to stop it from happening in the future?

They were seated and served drinks immediately. No one seemed to care what they ate, so Lucas ordered for them all— one of her favorite meals.

She wondered if it was coincidence or if he remembered she favored it. At the thought, she gently berated herself. Of course, he didn't remember.

Luckily, Rhys and Willow soon entered the room, and she didn't have to think about it further. "Have you ordered?" he asked.

"Just now." Lucas answered for the group.

"Good."

Rhys escorted Willow to the table, and as they took their seats, his hand lingered an extra moment on her stomach as if to remind her of the baby she carried. When Willow smiled reassuringly at her husband, Abby felt and ache in her heart.

She wanted that someday. A husband who cared for her, protected her, but didn't try to control her.

Catching her sister-in-law's attention, Willow smiled at Abby before she turned her attention to the new women. "I'm Willow, and I'm so happy to meet you all, even though the circumstances could be better. I'm sorry for what's happened. I don't know if you know much about me or my situation, but when I first arrived it was similar to yours. I came with a large group of unmarried women. And the men in town...let's just say they behaved similarly." She shook her head regretfully. "I want to assure you that this is not how it will always be. Things will calm down, and you'll all be able to lead great lives here."

"Thank you," Lily said. "I think I speak for all of us when I say I truly hope that's the case."

The others nodded.

Lucas took command of the situation. "Now that we're settled, we need to come to some decisions. What just happened out there cannot, under any circumstance, happen again. You ladies are integral in expanding the town, and I refuse to have you chased off. Rest assured, you'll be protected."

Rhys nodded in agreement. "None of you know me, but I'm Rhys Winthrop. Abby is my sister, and I own this hotel."

"We've heard of you before," Grace offered easily. "I think you'd have to be living under a rock for the last decade to not hear of your hotels."

He smiled, pleased. "What you probably don't know is that I take the protection of the people in my life very seriously."

Willow snorted and rolled her eyes playfully. "You can say that again."

The joke eased some of the tension in the room, and Abby was grateful. "I second that."

Rhys smiled, amused. "Yes, well, my point is you're not alone here."

"Exactly," Lucas said. "You're not alone. We've brought you here, and we're not abandoning you. Our number one goal is to get you all settled in positions you'll enjoy. Let me make this very clear: you are not required to marry. We never had that stipulation, and we never will. However, if you choose to do so, please do so with our blessing."

The women nodded again, but Charlotte lifted a finger to get everyone's attention. "We were speaking on the way here. Not all of us know what we'd like to do, but a few of us have ideas. Is it possible for us to choose our jobs, or will you place us somewhere to start, and then we'll change as desired after?"

Lucas nodded. "Excellent question. Ideally, we'd find you a position of your choosing. Something you'll enjoy. We want you to be happy here. And perhaps write home about how amazing it is so others will take the leap and join you."

More chuckles sounded, and Abby was surprised she'd laughed as well. Lucas was charming, more than he'd ever been in the past. When they were younger, he'd been brash, forthright, and would push until he got his way. He'd changed in that time, developed more than just his outward polish.

When everyone quieted down, he took command again, his tone more serious. "While all of that will happen—shortly —we need to diffuse the current situation first. There is no way we can find positions for you when your safety is in question."

Hannah frowned. "But how? I thought I'd gotten through to them, but it only took one comment for a riot to break out. These men aren't civilized."

Before Lucas could say something, Abby interrupted. "Oh, but they are. Please, give them a chance. I've been here for a year now. The men, while a little high spirited, are really quite gentle and charming. I've been courted by several of them, and they've behaved in complete, gentlemanly fashion. I won't lie. They aren't like the men back east. They're stronger and more passionate, but I think you'll come to find them to your liking."

Willow was smiling in agreement while Rhys looked amused as he eyed Lucas. Confused, she glanced at Lucas and found his posture rigid.

He cleared his throat. "Exactly. I think, if given the chance, these men will impress you. I know it isn't why you've come, but this town is full of millionaires. They're looking to establish themselves and start families, and you would each be very well taken care of if you decide to marry."

He glanced over at Abby, and her stomach flipped at the heat she saw there. There was no mistaking it. But when he blinked, it was gone.

She thought over what she'd said. He couldn't possibly be…jealous. Could he?

Lily waved off the idea of marrying well. " I would like to start my life here without delay. How do you suggest we go about calming them down?"

Abby bit her lip. "Well, I'm not sure if you're going to like this, but why don't we give them what they want?"

Hannah arched a brow. "What exactly do you mean? They want *us*," she said, as if Abby hadn't grasped that.

"Exactly. They want us. I sincerely doubt any amount of hiding is going to change that. What they need is to get to know you. To see that you aren't going to be snapped up like the last flapjack on the table."

Lucas and Rhys didn't appear to like her idea, but Willow nodded. "I agree. It's almost like what we had to do when we first got here. We allowed the men to court us, and while they competed with each other, we gave them ways to channel their enthusiasm. Since we were short on funds in the beginning, we even auctioned off picnic baskets we'd made. The winners got to eat with us. Let's just say, I never expected such high bids for my ham and cheese sandwiches." The women laughed, charmed at the idea. "The men really are wonderful, if you give them a chance."

Charlotte nodded, determination gleaming in her china-blue eyes. "I agree. Right now, we're shiny, new toys. Let's give them a chance to get used to us and for the frenzy to pass."

Lucas seemed to mull it over, but he finally agreed. "All right. I think it's the best plan at this point. Let's host a *controlled* gathering where the men can get to know you all. With any luck, after an evening of mingling, we can move forward with our business."

"Agreed," Rhys said. "May I suggest hosting it here? My staff can keep extra eyes on the women, and having it in the hotel will also reinforce manners."

Emery looked around. "What will we do? Talk the whole evening?" She looked less than thrilled. "Sounds exhausting."

Abby smiled. "It doesn't have to be like that."

"We could have a ball," Hannah suggested.

Grace's lips turned down. "I'm not a very good dancer."

A perfectly arched brow rose on Hannah's face. "We could practice."

Grace shuddered. "I'll pass."

"All right. No ball," Lily agreed.

Abby tapped her lip. "I think the problem is that it's overwhelming. Having the men's attention only on the five of you."

The women nodded quickly. "Exactly," Emery agreed. "I feel like I'm going to get cornered with no way out."

"Why don't we invite the rest of the town? Married couples and other single women. We could even do something where men and women are paired for, oh, three to five minutes, talk, and then change partners. It would move quickly, stay interesting, and hopefully, be less overwhelming." Willow suggested.

Charlotte bounced in her chair. "I like that idea. Seems a lot less intimidating."

"Agreed." Hannah inclined her head. "But I'm concerned the other women won't want to participate. I think we should require *all* unmarried persons to participate."

The others nodded their agreement before Grace looked thoughtfully at Abby. "You wouldn't mind, would you?"

"Not at all." She smiled brightly. She was happy to help in any way she could, and if it made them feel more comfortable to have her chatting with men right alongside them, she would gladly do it. "It sounds enjoyable."

Rhys nodded firmly. "Good. That's settled then. I think it's a good plan, and it'll accomplish what we need it to. I'll arrange for it to take place in a few days. The sooner the better." He looked to Lucas for confirmation, and when he nodded, Rhys continued. "However, I don't feel comfortable with you all alone at the house. I can't force you, but it would ease my mind if you would stay in the hotel." When Abby was about to object, he added, "Only until the event."

She would've immediately agreed to the request, but she wouldn't speak for the others. "What do you think?" she asked them.

Emery shrugged. "It seems the most logical course. We'll be safer here."

The others voiced their agreements, and Abby smiled. "Looks like we're staying here."

Hopefully, in a week, all of this would be over.

CHAPTER 7

The party was a smashing success and it was still early. Lucas stood at the entrance and greeted guests with Rhys while the women, dressed in their finery, mingled around the room.

Lucas caught a flute of champagne from a passing server as he nodded to another newcomer. Rhys had been right to suggest the hotel. He couldn't imagine getting the same elevated manners outdoors. The gleaming floors, the sparkling chandeliers, and the quartet, softly playing in the corner, all whispered of sophistication.

Men were taking turns with the ladies, and it appeared as though several married couples had stationed themselves close to the ladies as another form of protection. Lucas appreciated the gesture, and marveled that the community functioned so well, considering the imbalance between men and women.

The town was small, and everyone knew each other, that much was clear. But that would soon change as the copper mine began production. More men would be added to the mix, and Lucas wondered how things would change.

Abigail's laughter floated in the air, and the hairs on the back of his neck stood on end. He didn't look in her direction, just relished the sound, as he welcomed another guest into the ballroom.

Even now, he could picture the mint silk she wore molded to her body. It was shades lighter than the emeralds that graced her neck, but neither could compare to the hue of her eyes.

His own were brown. Like mud, he'd always thought. Except now he remembered Abby had said they were like brandy. Warm, rich, and inviting. He'd forgotten that. He'd forgotten so much. And he wondered if those things had slowly left his mind, or if he'd forced them out, knowing that if he remembered those moments—remembered *her*—he would have returned and begged her forgiveness, never to become the type of man she deserved.

He gulped the rest of his champagne and glanced in Abigail's direction. She was speaking with three men, all dressed in their finest suits, their adoring gazes all on her as she smiled and entranced them all.

He knew what that felt like, to be captivated by her. To get lost in her joy for life and the goodness she saw around her. It was heady, addicting, and he didn't blame those poor fools for an instant.

Rhys leaned closer to him. "Stop looking at her."

Amused, Lucas kept his face forward and placed his glass on a server's empty tray. "I was looking out at the room."

"No, you weren't. I might be helping you, but only because it'll protect Abby. Everything I said still stands."

He didn't disagree with Rhys—he wasn't going to force himself, or his company, on Abigail. But he hadn't expected the interest he felt toward her, and he was tired of Rhys telling him what to do. "I'll stay away as long as she wants me to."

When Rhys inhaled sharply, Lucas knew he'd hit his mark. Rhys wanted to protect Abby, but he wouldn't control her. Lucas wanted the same thing. "And now, I think it's about time we start the main event."

They walked farther in the room, and Lucas went to stand on a small platform, so everyone could see him. As he stepped on stage, the noise level in the room dropped. Lucas smiled. That never got old. When he'd been poor, a nobody, this never would have happened. It amazed him what money and power could do.

He waved for the quartet to take a break. "Thank you all for joining us this evening." He waited a moment for the applause to stop. "I hope you've been enjoying the delicious food the Promise Creek Hotel has provided for us, as well." More cheers sounded.

Everyone seemed pleased, and Lucas took it as a good sign. "Now, I know everyone is excited to welcome Promise Creek's newest residents." A few men let out whistles. "They are good-hearted ladies, looking to make their mark here, and I know you'll treat them as they deserve." The men sobered up, just as he'd hoped.

"Now, we thought it would be fun to play a little game to get to know each other better. Unfortunately for the married couples, this is just for the unwed guests tonight. We'll call it...quick courting." Someone in the crowd tittered. "We'll make two lines. One line of women, the other of men. We'll ring a bell every three minutes. During that time, talk to the person across from you, get to know your partner. Ask them what they like to eat, what their favorite activities are, anything polite you would like to know about them. After the three minutes are up, the bell will ring, and the men will move to the next lady on their right. We will continue to do this until each gentleman has had a chance to converse with each lady. How does that sound?"

Cheers erupted, and some of the other unmarried ladies in town giggled nervously, but they seemed eager.

"All right then! Everyone line up on the empty side of the room. There's no need to worry about where you're standing. Remember, everyone will have a chance to speak with each lady.

He moved with the crowd to the back of the room, hoping to set an example of proper behavior, and he was pleasantly surprised with how calm the crowd was. Perhaps Abby and Willow were right. With a little time to get to know the women, things would settle down.

He counted twenty-two unmarried ladies, and there were at least seven men for each woman. Inviting the rest of the town had been a stroke of genius.

He stood at the end of the line, making sure the men saw he wasn't trying to get ahead of them. When the first bell rang, the men around him talked good-naturedly with one another, patiently waiting their turn.

The conversations between the men and the women started hesitantly, but he noted the shyness quickly dissipated. By the sixth partner change, conversations—and laughter—began immediately.

"Who are you interested in?" the man next to him asked. He must not have recognized Lucas immediately. "Oops," he corrected himself. "Guess you're not interested like that." The man laughed. He seemed kind though. Sort of like a puppy.

Lucas grinned at the man. "All the women seem great."

"Oh, they are. There may not be many of them, but the ones we have sure are quality."

"What about you? Are you interested in any of the women? Some of the new arrivals, perhaps?"

"Well," the man stammered, "I've been courting someone seriously."

Lucas' eyebrows went up. "Really?" He looked over at the women to see if any of them were darting glances in the man's direction. He couldn't make out who the lucky lady might be. Although he didn't know the man well, he could tell he was kind and, from the looks of him, very well off.

"Yeah. I'm not the only one after her, but I think she favors me."

Lucas smiled at the thought. Things really weren't any different here. The women out east who were wealthy and beautiful were highly sought after. They had tens, if not hundreds, of suitors vying for their attention. It was the same here, except the only qualification a woman need have was to be unmarried. Looks and fortune, Lucas imagined, were optional. Although, if a woman *was* beautiful and wealthy, he imagined her potential suitors would amount to the whole town. "Which one?" He gestured to the line.

"The brunette on the far side. Prettiest green eyes you've ever seen."

All amusement faded. "You're courting Miss Winthrop?"

The man didn't appear to notice Lucas' mood. "Every chance she allows, I take her for a drive or a picnic or some such. Wish I was the only one though. She doesn't seem ready to commit. But I have a plan," he said with a conspirator's wink. "I'm hoping it'll win me a kiss."

"Is that so? What will you do?"

"Oh. I can't tell you that. Then word would get out, and someone else might do it."

He seemed so pleased with his idea, and all Lucas wanted to do was knock the smile off his face.

They'd been slowly moving forward, and now he was forced into conversation. It was easy enough to ask the lady a question and allow her to talk the rest of the time as he listened to the man interested in Abigail converse with each lady. He was polite, attentive, and a gentleman.

However, as the bell rang once more and he moved in front of Abigail, he lit up. "Abby, it's great to see you again."

Abigail chuckled. "You as well, Connor. I hope your finger healed."

The man held up his hand so she could see for herself. "Very well, thanks to your prompt attention."

She rewarded him with a smile.

It was then Lucas realized he hadn't started speaking with Lily, who was his current partner. When he brought his attention back to her, he tried to block out the inane chatter next to him. He coughed uncomfortably. "Forgive me, Miss Reed. I was distracted."

Her lake-blue eyes glanced over at Abigail. "Apparently."

Lucas wasn't one to blush, but he felt the temperature rise in his face. He hoped it didn't show.

Finally, she clucked. "This seems to be going very well," she said, mercifully.

"Yes." He looked down the line. Several of the women had run out of men to speak with and were escorted to the refreshment tables. "It's gone even better than I'd hoped. With any luck, next time you come into town, you'll receive a better welcome."

Lily rolled her eyes. "I'm just hoping the men leave us alone. I would hate to have to fend them off every time we need supplies."

He chuckled. "I'm sorry to disappoint you, but I think you'll receive attention wherever you go." He hadn't meant to compliment her, just speak the truth. She was a beautiful woman, one with striking looks, and red hair that looked like fire. Any man would be itching to touch it.

As if thinking the same thing, she reached up and fingered a curl. "I would've thought this would keep them away."

He laughed and leaned forward conspiratorially. "We redheads are an interesting lot. There aren't many who can ignore us."

That surprised a laugh from her, and her eyes were smiling with merriment when the bell rang.

Lily had distracted him so much he'd forgotten he was speaking with Abigail—Abby—next. And when he looked at her, she was glancing between him and Lily, a notch between her brows.

The smile fell from his face as he moved two steps over. "Hi," he said, almost immediately cursing himself for that brilliant opener.

"Hi."

It suddenly seemed a little hotter in the room, and the urge to tug on his collar was overwhelming, but he held still and tried to relax. Three minutes. He could do this. "Have you been enjoying the quick courtings?"

A small smile quirked her lips, and his eyes were drawn to them. He could almost remember what she tasted like.

"It's been interesting. It was a great idea."

He agreed. "Are you planning to return to the house tonight?"

She shook her head, and a thick, glossy brown curl fell from her coiffure. "No, Rhys thought it best to stay one more night. I agree with him. Hopefully when we leave tomorrow, everything will have settled."

"I think it will."

"It'll be nice to get back to real life." She laughed with a hint of self-depreciation. "It's been quiet for most of the last year. I'm not used to all this excitement."

He suddenly wanted to know about everything that had happened since he left her all those years ago. What had her life been like? How long had she waited before courting others? "How did you and Rhys end up in Promise Creek?" The words were out of his mouth before he could stop them.

"Oh." Her shoulders fell a little, and she nibbled on that delicious lip like she couldn't decide whether to tell him or not. "Well, I ran away. I ended up here by myself, with hardly any money." She shook her head. "The owner of this hotel, the one before Rhys," she clarified, "even threw me out on the street."

Ice filled his veins at the image she wove. She'd run away from home. With nothing. No protection. And ended up in a town where she was at the mercy of everyone around her. "What happened after...after you were thrown out?" His mouth was so dry, he almost couldn't finish the sentence.

"Willow found me right as I was kicked out. She took me under her wing. Gave me a place to live. Soon after, Rhys tracked me down. He was determined to bring me home." She chuckled at the memory. "But you know what it's like to try and get me to do something I don't want to do."

He smiled, but when her eyes met his, the humor left her face.

"Abby—"

She gasped and looked at him with shock.

"Forgive me. I've been hearing everyone call you that."

"No. It's all right. It's what I prefer. I'm different now. I'm not the Abigail that lived in Manhattan."

He nodded slowly. "I can see that. A lot has changed." And yet, so much had stayed the same. She was still the most beautiful, most compelling woman he'd ever met. He still respected her, appreciated her humor and her spirit, and more than anything, adored that she protected those she cared about. But he didn't say any of that. Instead, he took in a deep breath. "I owe you an apology."

She shook her head. "No."

"Yes. I do. How I left was wrong."

She was still shaking her head, but she didn't tell him to be quiet.

"I knew you didn't agree with me about why we wouldn't work, and instead of trying to make you see, I decided it was best to leave. Best for both of us. That was wrong. I shouldn't have done that. You deserved a choice too."

She finally looked at him. Really looked at him, like she could see deep inside, from who he'd been to who he was now. Finally she opened her mouth to respond—

And the bell rung.

Their time was up.

She closed her lips and gave him a final nod, just as the next man tapped his shoulder. There was so much more he wanted to say, so much more he wanted to discuss. But he'd done the one thing he should have done long ago. He'd apologized.

It just wasn't enough.

CHAPTER 8

Abby was a nervous wreck as they drove into town two days after the soiree at the hotel. They all were. They'd spoken very little, only going over the plan Lucas and Rhys had devised for if another mob broke out.

But that wouldn't happen, she assured herself. Lucas and Rhys would be there to oversee their first arrival.

She knew everything was going to go smoothly, but it was hard to erase what had happened last time. "All right. So, what are everyone's plans when we get into town?" she asked, just a bit too cheerfully.

There was a moment's hesitation before Charlotte decided to play along. "I'm going to see if there are any buildings available for a bakery. Perhaps ask around to see if such a place would be welcome."

Abby knew a bakery would be well received by all the residents of Promise Creek. "I think you'll hear little argument over having another place to get quality food."

Charlotte grinned. "Exactly what I'm hoping for."

Emery and Grace were going shopping while Lily wandered and explored. Hannah planned to spend time in the hotel's library, a place she'd grown attached to during their stay.

"What about you?" Lily asked. "What are your plans?"

Truthfully, she hadn't any. Her plan was to get the women into town, make sure they were all safe, and then...she had no idea. She'd probably pay someone a visit or poke her nose into the hotel's business. Rhys would just *love* that.

The women lapsed into silence again as they neared the edge of town, their nervousness escalating. But as they turned onto the main road, one of the men from the other evening raised his hat as they passed. "Good morning, Miss Winthrop, ladies."

Charlotte and Grace waved, while the rest of them nodded. "Good morning," they said almost in unison.

Hannah shoulders relaxed slightly. "Well, that was friendly. Let's just hope the others behave similarly."

As they entered the town square, it was as if the mob the week before had never happened. Men called out to them, waving enthusiastically and addressing either the whole group or shouting individual greetings. Although this was much more attention than Abby was used to, the behavior was back to normal, and that relieved her.

She saw Lucas and Rhys waiting for her at the mercantile, and after she parked, only a few more greetings were tossed their way.

Rhys looked relieved, but Lucas was harder to read. Both men stepped forward, their postures looser than when she'd seen them last, as they helped each lady out of the wagon.

Charlotte happily placed her fists on her hips and blew out an exaggerated breath now that she was safely on solid ground. "Well, that went much better than expected." The rest of the women let out chuckles of relief.

Lucas smiled. "Much better than last time, I agree. Now that we're here, what are your plans? Normally, I would never ask such a thing, but for the next few times you come into town, I'd like to know so I can make sure you're safe."

Each of the women vocalized what they would like to do, and Lucas nodded. "Would any of you like an escort?"

Emery shook her head. "I appreciate the offer, but I'd like to start out how I plan on continuing." She looked around at the group. "I can't speak for everyone, but that is what I'd like."

Lily nodded her quick agreement, and while Grace and Charlotte agreed, they also decided to walk together for added safety. All eyes turned to Hannah, and she lowered her head a bit too demurely. "I would like an escort. I was overconfident last time, and it got me into trouble."

While her request made sense, it needled Abby. Did she truly feel unsafe, or was she trying to rope Lucas into spending time with her? And even if she was, why did Abby care? Lucas didn't belong to her. He never had.

"Good." Abby clapped her hands. "It's settled then. We'll meet back here in three hours, unless any of you feel you need more time." She looked around the group, but everyone seemed happy. "Enjoy." Her smile was tight.

Abby turned to the horses, but Rhys intervened. "Let my employees handle them."

Normally, she'd be happy to, but she had nothing else to do right then, and she desperately wanted something to occupy her mind. But seeing no way to refuse without looking ridiculous, she gave her brother another overly bright smile and thanked him.

His eyes narrowed, and he looked at her closely. "Is everything all right? You aren't worried, are you?"

His genuine concern soothed some of her frustration, and her shoulders deflated. "Not at all. Everything is all right." Her eyes strayed toward Lucas, but she quickly averted them.

Unfortunately, not quickly enough.

Now Rhys was looking between the two of them and didn't look happy in the slightest. At least Lucas didn't notice —he was too busy talking with Hannah.

"Abby—"

She shook her head, refusing to talk about it. "I'm fine," she stressed again. She looked past Rhys to Hannah and Lucas. "I'll see you later."

Hannah nodded happily and turned back to Lucas, but before she could speak, Rhys placed himself between them. "If you follow me, Miss Pierce, we'll fetch you an escort."

Abby had just turned around, but Rhys' words had her glancing back.

Hannah's straightened quickly. "But I thought..." She glanced at Lucas.

Lucas raised a brow. "Is something wrong?" He appeared as if he had no idea what Hannah wanted, but Abby knew Lucas would never be so obtuse. He knew what Hannah was after and was handily extricating himself from the situation.

She wasn't sure why, but Abby felt an immense amount of happiness over that. She shouldn't care who Lucas spent his time with, but as much as she tried to fight it, she did. The whole situation was so confusing. Why couldn't this be simple?

She wasn't in love with Lucas anymore, and she needed to allow both of them to move on with their lives.

Hannah quickly recovered, and her lips quirked with a contented smile. "No, of course not. Thank you for your consideration." She nodded politely at Rhys. "Please, lead on."

As if realizing that Abby would be left alone with Lucas, Rhys looked between the two of them, then settled his gaze on Abby. "Will you be all right?"

She wasn't sure, if she were being honest, but she nodded

encouragingly at her brother. "I'll be fine. I think I'll pay Aria a visit while I'm here."

"Let me know if you need anything." He glanced meaningfully in Lucas' direction.

"Of course."

At one point, she'd been tired of Rhys' overbearing attitude, but now she was grateful for it. He was only protective because he loved her so much.

Abby waved one last time as Rhys led Hannah to the hotel. She watched them a little longer than necessary, but the alternative was to give her attention to Lucas, who remained beside her.

Realizing he wasn't going to leave, she took a deep breath, and looked at him with what she hoped was confidence. "Thank you for meeting us. The others were nervous, but knowing you two would be waiting helped alleviate some fears."

"I'm glad. I want to help in any way I can." He looked at her meaningfully.

She did her best not to read into anything. He wasn't saying he wanted to help *her*. He was being kind, and she couldn't fault him for that. He was doing his job. Plain and simple.

She smiled, hoping it looked genuine. "Thank you. I'm sure the others know that as well."

"Abby..." he said, drawing out her name.

Hearing him say her name filled her with a longing she didn't want. She swallowed hard, then forced herself to meet his eyes. "Have a wonderful day, Mr. McDermott."

She didn't allow him to respond as she turned and left.

CHAPTER 9

Lucas wasn't sure what had just happened. He'd felt as though he'd made progress with Abby, but if the conversation just now was any indication, he was failing miserably.

He watched her walk away, her hips gently swaying with each step, her back rigid like she knew he watched her. He should turn away, go somewhere else, attend to some of his other business, but he couldn't seem to rip his gaze away.

Abby was the only person to ever fill his heart, and even though that was years ago, he was starting to realize that some of his feelings remained. If he were a good man, he would leave her alone and allow her to find peace here. Perhaps find another man.

But Lucas wasn't that good, and as he watched her leave, he realized one important truth: he wanted Abby back in his life, even if it was only as a friend. He just hoped it would be enough.

She continued down the street, and eventually opened the front gate to one of the large houses near the bank on Main Street. The front yard was large and filled with cascading flowers in full bloom. Two children ran around screaming, playing some sort of game. Abby gave them both hugs before continuing up to the porch.

The sight tugged at his heart. He tried to live his life without regrets. He dealt honestly, he treated his workers fairly, and he never swindled anyone. Because of that, he'd been proud of what he'd built. But now, he wasn't proud of how it had started out, of how he'd left Abby.

Seeing her with those children, he realized it could've been his life. It could've been *their* life. He'd thought he had to leave to earn his fortune, that only then he'd be worthy of her. Now he wondered if he could have built his empire while married to her. It would've been harder, and he wouldn't have had the unlimited hours he'd dedicated toward it, but he still could have done it.

He'd sacrificed the only person he'd cared about, the only person he'd loved, because of pride.

Disgust filled him, and he turned away. He'd ruined things between them, and there was no one to blame but himself.

He walked several steps before looking back over his shoulder one last time. He saw Abby run back down the porch steps and round the house instead of walking through the front door.

Before he even realized it, he was jogging toward the house. Had something happened? Worry filled him as he approached and heard squeals echoing from the backyard. He panicked and raced around the side of the house.

But when he reached the back, he heard laughter mixed with the screams, and he stumbled to a stop at the scene in front of him.

Chickens scurried in a panic as a black puppy terrorized them. He looked more closely and realized the dog wasn't trying to hurt them, just get them riled up.

The children ran into the madness, and Abby jumped in

along with a woman with flaming red hair. They attempted to gather the chickens, only to end up laughing when the offended birds squawked and batted their wings until they got away.

The other woman puffed out a breath that set a curl flying. "Drat, you good-for-nothing birds. Get back here!" The woman's Irish accent rang clearly through the air. "Go that way, Abby! We'll corner 'em!"

Abby positioned herself at the far end, and they both charged the bird. The Irish woman caught the chicken, but the two women laughed so hard, the chicken got away, and they dissolved into a fit of giggles on the grass.

Lucas approached the group and towered over the women as he came into their view. He raised a brow in amusement. "May I be of assistance in your chicken hunting?"

Abby's face lost some of its color, and her smile fled, but the other woman dissolved into another fit of giggles. Abby stood up quickly and pulled her friend up with her.

The stranger smiled at him as she dusted feathers off her skirt. "Forgive me. I'm Aria Grant."

He bowed his head formally. "Lucas McDermott." He darted a quick glance at Abby, his lips quirked with amusement "One of the Copper Kings."

Her eyes widened. "Oh! Please forgive me. As you can see, we're having a bit of difficulty."

He rocked back on his heels. "A chicken malfunction, I see."

Abby snorted, and he felt a flush of satisfaction. "Something like that."

Lucas looked at the dog still causing havoc. "Is that your pet?"

Mrs. Grant's moss-green eyes narrowed playfully at the dog. "Aye, he's our mongrel. He needs extensive training, obviously."

Lucas laughed. "You'll manage it. In the meantime, would you like help gathering the chickens?"

Abby's mouth fell open, and her eyes darted to his. "You're going to chase chickens?"

Her shock and disbelief only made the moment sweeter. He shrugged, trying to hide his amusement. "It won't be my first time."

Mrs. Grant waved him away. "Thank you, but we wouldn't want to trouble you. I'm sure you have more important things to attend to."

"It would be my pleasure. It's been some time since I've had such an opportunity."

Mrs. Grant's eyes wrinkled with her smile. "Thank you, then. I'll just take this pariah into the house," she said, as she took hold of the puppy and wrangled him away from the chaos.

Abby shifted on her feet uneasily, and he could tell she was uncomfortable having him there. But they really did need his help if they wanted to catch the chickens anytime soon. As it was, the hens were so riled they wouldn't lay eggs for days.

Lucas walked back to the porch, shrugging out of his jacket, folding it in half, and laying it over the banister. He undid his cuffs and rolled the fine material up to his elbows.

Abby eyed his exposed skin as if in a trance. Unable to help himself, he flexed his muscles, and watched as fascination filled her eyes before she jerked her head away and swallowed. Without saying anything else, she started chasing her first chicken.

He watched in amusement as she only terrorized the bird further. He moved and quickly scooped up a hen, placing it back in the pen.

Abby huffed out a breath and put her hands on her hips. "How did you do that?"

"I told you, I have a lot of practice."

She shook her head, finally laughing. "Just show us," she said as Aria returned.

He didn't need to be asked twice. He instructed them on the correct way to approach the hens, how to grab them, and how to hold them securely before releasing them.

After the short lesson, they quickly gathered the rest of the chickens, and then walked back to the porch to collect Lucas' coat. Mrs. Grant smiled at him. "Thank you for your help, Mr. McDermott. I'm afraid it would've taken us much longer, if ever, to collect them all."

He laughed. "I'm glad I was able to be of assistance. You can call me anytime you need help gathering chickens."

Mrs. Grant shook her finger playfully at him. "You better be careful. I might just take you up on that, and then you'd be gathering my hens every day."

He shrugged back into his coat. "The exercise will be very beneficial to my health."

Abby shook her head at him, like she would an errant child. "Don't encourage him, Aria."

Aria glanced between the two of them. "Do you know each other?"

He cocked his head but remained silent, watching as Abby stammered, realizing her mistake. "We knew each other from back home. A long time ago."

Was that all he was to her? Someone from her past? Regret filled him again.

Aria smiled, but Lucas could tell she wasn't fully convinced. There was too much tension between them. "I see."

Abby winced, but didn't say anything more. Awkward silence enveloped the group.

Aria shook her head. "Well, in any case, I'm grateful both of you stopped by to help."

"Oh! We aren't together. At least, we didn't walk here together." Abby frowned and looked at Lucas. "Why *are* you here?"

"I saw you run back here, and then I heard screams. I was concerned someone was injured."

Aria beamed. "A Copper King and a hero as well."

Lucas tipped his hat. "Always willing to oblige."

Abby cleared her throat. "Anyway, the other ladies wanted to explore town, so we all came in together, but I didn't have any plans. I thought a visit might be nice, if you're available."

Aria reached out and took Abby's hand. "That's right! Was it better today? You weren't mobbed again were you?" Worry tinged her voice.

Abby squeezed before releasing Aria's hand. "It was much better. The quick courtings seem to have worked. The men were friendly today, but they didn't approach us."

Aria heaved a sigh of relief. "Good. We were so worried when we heard about what had happened."

Lucas nodded. "Rest assured that something like that will never happen again. We'll be more prepared for the next group that comes in."

Abby smiled tightly as though she wasn't sure what else to do. "Are you free this afternoon?" she asked Aria.

"Yes. Yes of course—" Aria groaned. "Wait. I'm not. I forgot I have a meeting about refurbishing the church."

Lucas' ears perked up. "What are you doing with the church?"

"It's a bit...shabby, if it's all right to say so." She grimaced. "It always feels wrong to criticize the Lord's house, but it's true. It was originally built by a bunch of roughneck miners. Great for what it was intended for, but now that the town is growing, it needs some repairs and updating."

"I look forward to seeing what you ladies come up with. If there's anything you need help with, anything at all, please ask me. These are the type of things my partners and I like to assist with."

Aria beamed. "That's most thoughtful of you, Mr. McDermott." She elbowed Abby. "This man's a good one."

Abby spluttered, but Aria didn't seem to notice. "Anyway, I need to get going." She turned to Abby. "I'm sorry we couldn't have our visit. Come back soon—I want to hear everything that's happened. And bring the new women," she added enthusiastically.

"I will."

They waved goodbye, and Lucas held the front gate open for Abby as they made their way back to Main Street. They walked in silence toward the town square as Lucas racked his brain for something to say. Everything he tried out in his mind sounded inane. Finally, he asked, "What will you do now?"

She didn't seem to mind the small talk. "I'm not sure, actually," she admitted. "I could visit someone else, but I'm assuming most everyone will be busy with the church planning. I should probably talk to Rhys or get a bite to eat in the hotel."

Lucas wasn't hungry, but the thought of sharing a meal with her, of having her attention for a little while, was too good to pass up.

"Abby," he said, pausing near a towering rosebush. She stopped as well, but he could see the reluctance in her eyes. "Look, I know I said it the other night, but I am really sorry for how things ended between us." She wouldn't meet his gaze, but he had to get the rest out. "I know I have no right to say this or to ask you this, but I must. Seeing you has brought back so many memories of who I once was. I've changed so much, have done so much, but part of me wants to get back just a little of my past. We cared about one another, but more than anything, we were friends. The closest of friends."

He paused, allowing her to respond. She finally nodded, unable to deny it. "What do you want, Lucas?"

Warmth filled him. "I would like us to be friends again, if at all possible. If not, if you don't want anything to do with me, I'll stay away from you. But I would really like the opportunity to be your friend. I'm in charge of the women, which means I'll be at the house a lot. I would like it to not be awkward between us."

She looked away again. "And is that all? You want to be friends so it's easier to do business when I'm around?"

"No," he said firmly. "I want to be your friend. I want to know who you are now, because no matter how long it's been, I still care."

She looked at him warily, and he didn't blame her in the slightest. He'd lost her trust, he'd hurt her. Anyone would be a fool to give history the opportunity to repeat itself. But the Abigail he knew, the woman he'd loved, had been forgiving. And he wondered if there was any part of her that still cared for him.

She kept looking at him as if sifting through her feelings and weighing the risks, but finally she blew out a long breath and nodded slowly. "All right. I should probably be put in an asylum for this, but I would like that. I, too, don't want this to be awkward, and there's no denying that it is now."

Relief filled him. She could change her mind at any time, but for now, she was agreeing to it. "Would you like to have lunch with me?"

Her eyes widened. "I beg your pardon?"

He grinned then. "You did say we could be friends."

"Yes, but"—she waved her hands around—"I didn't think we'd immediately start dining together."

"No time like the present."

"Apparently not."

"I noticed some of your favorites on the menu at the hotel."

She bit her lip. "I know. Every time I'm in town, I gorge." She laughed. "It's too hard to resist." *He had remembered!*

He offered her his arm. "Then shall we?"

Her mouth dropped open. "You can't be serious! You want to go to the hotel—where Rhys is. You must be crazy."

"Rhys shouldn't have a problem with it," he said confidently.

She snorted. "Now I see how little you know my brother."

"I'm serious. Even if he doesn't like it, he'll have to be fine with it. He told me to stay away from you unless you chose otherwise."

She lost her smile. "When did you talk to him?"

"Almost the minute I stepped into the hotel that first day."

She groaned. "I knew it would be bad, but I didn't expect him to threaten you."

"He's your brother. I expected it. If you were my sister, I would've beaten me."

That brought a small smile to her face. "Still. He's not going to like it."

"Does it matter if he likes it or not?"

She chewed her lip as she thought it over. "No, but I'd rather not upset him. He'll worry."

Lucas wanted to take her to the hotel and buy her a meal she'd love, but if it was uncomfortable for her, they could do something else. "Is there anywhere else you would like to go? I saw a café. Is it any good?"

"It is. Sally's an excellent cook, but..."

"But?"

She shuffled her feet. "As much as I worry over Rhys' reaction, I do want to go to the hotel. Plus, if we are going to be *friends,*" she said the word strangely, like it was a foreign word she couldn't quite grasp, "he'll have to get used to seeing us together. Or at least, spending time together," she corrected.

"True." He offered her his arm again, and this time she slowly slipped her hand through it. The way it felt, the right-ness of it, was almost too much. It was such a small gesture, but it sent waves of pleasure through him.

Whatever he had to do, whatever he had to face, it was worth it for this. He just hoped she felt the same.

CHAPTER 10

I'm insane. I've gone mad. Those thoughts continually ran through Abby's mind as they neared the hotel.

It was possible to slip by Rhys, to go into the dining area and eat a meal without him ever knowing they were there. Possible, but not likely.

She softly groaned, hoping Lucas wouldn't hear. She was her own person, and Rhys supported that, but he wouldn't accept this easily. He wouldn't condone her spending time with the man who'd broken her heart, who'd changed the direction of her entire life. And she didn't blame him.

What am I doing?

Her hand instinctively clenched his forearm, and he flexed the muscle under her hand. The feeling sent tingles throughout her body, and she viscerally remembered their embraces and kisses from the past.

It'd been like that back then too. Like every time they touched, they'd ignite an explosion too massive to contain.

As they stepped up to the hotel's entrance, he placed his hand over hers a moment before releasing her. She stepped inside, a guilty flush rising up her neck as she looked around, expecting Rhys to spot her at any moment.

She knew she should allow Lucas to escort her to the dining room, but she couldn't stand the slow pace any longer. She was jittery. So instead of waiting for him, she quickly made her way to the dining room.

Lucas followed closely, and once the maître d' spotted them together, he whisked them to a secluded table off to the side, with plants discreetly placed to block the other diners' view.

Abby was seated quickly, and she looked up at the man. "Thank you, Hodgkins. This is exactly what we needed."

The man smiled, pleased. "Of course, miss. Anything for you."

Lucas nodded his thanks before taking his own seat. "Do you sit at this table often?"

She chuckled. "No. I've never needed to. I have a table saved across the dining room. No one sits there but me. Well, sometimes Willow."

"The privileges of being the owner's sister."

She draped her napkin over her lap. "Something like that."

"I would've thought your suitors brought you to the hotel for dinner."

Color rose to her cheeks, and she didn't quite meet his eyes. "They have."

It was his own fault for asking, but jealousy quickly whipped through him. He knew she hadn't kept herself hidden at home all these years. It was good she'd moved on, had gotten to know other men. He just wondered how she felt now—if there was anyone special. He had a feeling that if he asked, the meal would end immediately. And he wasn't willing to risk that. "I see," he said.

She didn't elaborate, and he didn't ask for more details.

"I know this might be awkward at first, but I refuse to feel guilty about what I've done," she said.

He shook his head vehemently. "You have nothing to feel sorry about."

"I know." She let out another breath and then laughed softly, but there was no humor in it. "Are we fooling ourselves, thinking this can work?"

His fingers itched to reach out and take her hand. But instead, he curled them into a ball in his lap. "No. We're not fooling ourselves. We were once friends. *Good* friends. We can get back there."

She shook her head, uncertain. "I don't know. That was so long ago. We were both different people." She eyed him. "You don't even look the same. Your hair is longer, more stylish. Your clothes are expensive, impeccable, and I know the cost of those cuff links." She smiled ruefully. "The Lucas from long ago didn't look like this."

Irritation tickled him. But it wasn't because of her, it was because of him. "The Lucas you knew was dirt poor. He was unworthy of you. He was bright," he said, "but he had little else."

"He had my love," she said, defiantly. "Was that not enough?"

His nostrils flared. "I wasn't good enough for you. Did you think I wanted to take advantage of your love? Take you away from everything you'd always known and force you into a life of poverty?"

Her face turned mutinous. "I could've done it. I would've been fine."

"I don't know. And I will never know. But have you ever gone hungry, Abby? Have you ever eaten flour infested with mealworms? Have you ever eaten scraps other workers threw away because you're so hungry it's either that or starve?"

"That would've never happened to us." Her voice was firm.

He shrugged. "I hope not. I hope that even if we didn't have the best place to live, or nice clothes, I'd still be able to provide food and a clean home. Those small things are luxuries to most people."

She remained silent for a moment, before nodding thoughtfully. "I know what you're saying, and I know you feel you did the right thing. I can't fault you for that, and honestly it was so long ago it doesn't really matter. I've never been hungry or dirty or any of the other things you imagine might have happened. I've seen those things. I know people who live like that. I do my best to help, but I truly believe we would've never ended up that way." She held up her hands and let them fall slowly. "It's in the past."

She was right. It *was* in the past. He needed to let it go, but for some reason every time he was with her, it was all he could think of. *What if.* What if he'd made a different choice? "I'm sorry."

She gave him a small smile. "I imagine interacting with each other like this is going to take some getting used to."

"You're right."

Sensing a lull in their conversation, the waiter came over and took their orders. Lucas snorted after the man left. "I could've ordered your lunch from memory."

"*Some* things haven't changed."

He certainly hoped not. He took a sip of the water the waiter had brought them, the cold beverage was refreshing, bracing even. "So, there's something I've been meaning to ask you."

"Hmm?"

He set down his glass and met her gaze. "Why did you run away? You told me some of it, but I want to know everything."

She shifted in her chair and laughed uneasily. "It's still a long story."

He held up his hands and gestured around the dining room. "We have all afternoon."

"True." She sighed. "All right. I'll tell you, but I'm not exactly proud of how it happened. To be honest, I'm a little embarrassed."

That surprised him. "Why?"

"Well... I was a little naïve."

It was a good thing he hadn't taken a drink right then. It might have come up his nose. "You *were?*" He knew he shouldn't have said it like that, but looking at her, all clean and elegant, looking fresh like a rose, she still looked innocent. And while he didn't doubt she'd seen some of the world, that innocence remained.

She narrowed her eyes at him, and he had the distinct feeling that if they'd been served bread, she would have torn off a piece and thrown it at his head. Laughing, he held up his hands as a gesture of peace. "Forgive me."

She scoffed. "You're not sorry." But she rolled her eyes playfully.

"So, why did you leave?"

After a moment's pause, she said, "Rhys and my mother told me it was time to marry."

Her statement was like a punch to the gut. "They were trying to force you into a marriage?"

She shrugged like it didn't matter, but he knew it must have. "It wasn't all that bad. I had my choice of *who* to marry. At least, if the person would have me."

Now it was Lucas' turn to scoff. "I can't imagine any man rejecting you."

She arched a brow at him. "Can't you?"

When he'd left her, he thought he'd been making the right choice for both of them. He thought over what he could say, how he could explain, but instead he remained quiet.

As the silence became awkward, she winced. "I'm sorry."

"If you need to lash out, you can. It's all right."

"No. It's not all right." She squeezed her eyes shut. "I think, more than anything, I'm upset with myself. I'm fine. Truly. I have been for years. Did it hurt when you left me? Of course. I was devastated, and it took a long time to get over it. But I'm fine now. There's no reason I should snap at you."

"All the same, you're allowed."

She shook her head in disbelief. "I forgot how persistent you could be."

"I'm probably even worse now, to be honest."

"Heaven help me." She took a sip of water. "I can safely say, I never thought I'd be in this situation. Here, talking with you. It's a little strange."

"I agree."

"Perhaps a little more than strange."

He leaned back in his chair. They were finally getting to a point where they weren't bashing up against each other. "Even more strange than the party you went to at the Oscar Mansion?"

Amusement twinkled in her eyes. "I'd forgotten about that."

"How does one forget that? A zebra ran across the yard right as she started her solo performance."

"I thought that old hen was going to convulse into connip —" Her hand shot out, gripping his as all amusement drained from her face.

He stilled. "What's wrong?"

He started to look over his shoulder, but she squeezed his hand. "Don't look."

Instinctively, he loosened his body, readying himself for anything. "What is it?" His voice was calm.

Her head jerked sideways so she could look over his shoulder. She sucked in a breath. "It's Rhys," she hissed.

That's what this was about? "All right. Is there a problem?"

She looked at him as if he lost his mind. "A problem? I'm having a meal with you! If he sees us, he'll be furious."

Lucas shook his head slowly. "I don't think so. When I spoke with him before—"

"He's coming this way!" She stood from her chair, yanking him up with her.

"What are we doing?" He tried to keep the amusement from his voice.

Again, she looked at him as if he were daft. "We have to hide."

"From Rhys?" He looked around at the sparse fronds, wondering where she would have them hide. "Would you like me to pretend to be a tree?"

"No! Just hide!"

He gestured around. "I don't know if you realized this, but there's nowhere to go."

Rhys moved in their direction, and Abby sprang into action. She dove behind the half wall with ferns above it, dragging him with. "There's a closet over there. We have to get there before he sees us."

"A closet?" He couldn't hold the amusement from his voice any longer.

"Yes!"

Although he didn't think Rhys would react that poorly to them dining together, he followed her. He was amused, and he wanted to see how far she would take this.

She opened the door and started pushing him in, all while keeping track of Rhys. She quickly jumped in after him, pressing herself against him, and closed the door quietly.

The closet was cramped, full of buckets and mops, with little empty space. He placed his hands against opposite walls, keeping his balance, but also keeping himself from reaching out and holding her.

Her breaths were short and shallow, and he felt every single one like a lash against him. He pushed his fingers against the walls, but it didn't help his desire to touch her. He wanted to wrap his arms around her, to pull her even tighter into him.

His breath stirred the wisps at her neck, and the scent of apples and vanilla filled his senses. His eyes rolled back into his head.

She kept shifting around, but all she succeeded in doing was brushing up against him. He groaned softly.

"Are you all right?" She asked him softly, throwing him a quick glance over her shoulder.

"Just fine." His voice sounded gravelly.

Taking him at his word, she looked back at the door, like she expected Rhys to come through at any moment. "We'll be out of here in a minute." She shifted again.

Cursing softly, he grabbed her, clamping his hands on her hips, holding her still.

She froze.

Even knowing he shouldn't, he leaned forward and inhaled deeply. Her scent was as potent as any drug. "If you don't stop moving around, I'm going to embarrass myself."

It was dim in the closet, but there was enough light coming in through the cracks to see a slight flush color her neck. In a trance, he brushed his lips over her feather-soft skin.

She sucked in a breath, but when he did it again, she moaned.

He knew he should stop, should pull away and let her go, but it was like a spell had been cast over him. He was powerless against the feelings coursing through him, and unless she told him to release her, he couldn't.

He skimmed his lips up to her ear, nibbling slightly just the way she liked. A tremor moved through her, but she still didn't tell him to stop. So he shifted to the other side, giving it equal attention.

"Lucas..." She said his name in a whispered moan.

Wanting to hear her say it again, he focused on where she liked it the most until he could hardly see straight. He whipped her around, pulling her flush against him. The contact sent electricity through their bodies, and her mouth formed an "o" as she closed her eyes.

"I'm not sure this is such a good idea," she whispered.

He moved one of his hands up to her neck, cradling the back of her head and forcing her gaze to meet his. "It's not. But I have to know." He had to know how she felt, how she tasted, if it felt the same—or even better than before. But he wouldn't force a kiss from her. He wouldn't take that choice away from her.

He saw a moment's indecision before her passion took over and she leaned forward. "I want to know too."

Her words lit a fuse in him, and he wrapped his arm tight around her waist, securing her, as his head swooped low, capturing her. The first taste of her soft lips, and the gasp she gave, was like coming home.

It was bliss.

White-hot light burst behind his eyes and his reason turned off. All he could do was feel. As if needing the same, she opened to him, taking as she gave, tasting as he devoured her.

They moved in sync, instinctively knowing and remembering how they fit together. And they still did. They fit perfectly after all the years they'd been apart, and the time fell away.

Her hands moved up his chest to his neck, finally settling in his hair, and shivers raced through him. His hair had been a lot shorter when they were together, but he'd never cut it short again after this. He wanted her to hold on as he brought them both pleasure.

Her chest rose and fell in quick succession, brushing tantalizingly against him, and all he could think about was how it would feel to have nothing between them.

The thought jarred him, and he pulled back from her, momentarily confusing the past and present. She was even more beautiful now than she'd been back then. Her girlhood had matured into womanhood, and the effect was stunning.

All he wanted to do was lean forward, take her lips again, and forget everything else. The past, the present, the future. Just enjoy the moment, enjoy her and that glazed, passion-filled look she'd had a moment ago before realizing where they were and, more importantly, what they were doing.

Her eyes cleared, and a notch formed between her brows. He ran his hands up and down her back, hoping to calm her, to reassure her.

If she could, he knew she would have stepped away from him, but in the closet, it wasn't possible. When she attempted it regardless of the cramped space, he held on. "Easy. If you step wrong, the buckets will alert everyone to where we are."

The thought of discovery held her still. "What are we doing, Lucas?"

He wished he had a good answer, wished he could tell her something that would make her feel better. But all that came to mind was *being together*. And he realized that's exactly what he wanted. He wanted to be with her. More than just friends, more than just acquaintances.

He'd thought being friends would be enough for him, but it wasn't. He needed more from her, and he wanted her to need that as well.

"Please let me go," she finally said, and he released her

immediately. No matter what he wanted, she was in charge. He would go at whatever pace she set, take only what she was willing to give him.

"Abby—"

She placed her finger over his lips, and he kissed it softly. She lowered her hand. "Please, don't say anything now. I need to think about all this. About what it means."

"It only has to mean whatever you want it to."

"That's the thing," she said softly, "I don't know what I want anymore."

CHAPTER 11

The minute Abby heard Lucas' voice downstairs in the entry of their home, she fled down the back stairs and out the kitchen door to the stables.

As she swiftly saddled a horse, she kept replaying what had happened between them at the hotel, same as she had for the last two days. Every touch, every kiss, every breath tormented her.

She pulled the cinch a little too tight and murmured her apology to Freckles, her horse, before loosening it. She was being ridiculous right now. She knew that, but she didn't care.

She had to get away—away from Lucas, from the memories, from the confusion. It was all too much.

She'd thought they could be friends, but she'd been wrong. There was too much history between them, too much chemistry for that to ever work.

Oh, that kiss... She closed her eyes tightly as she finished readying her mount. It would take her years to forget, if she even could.

Without wasting another moment, she climbed into the saddle and urged Freckles forward. Fresh air enveloped her, and the bands around her heart loosened. She knew she'd have to face Lucas to talk about what had happened, but she couldn't do it today. Not now.

She rounded the house, inhaling deeply, before ending on a gasp. Lucas was on the porch, watching her. Their eyes met, and her stomach flipped over. Without thinking, she launched Freckles into a gallop.

Abby tried to look away, but her eyes stayed glued to Lucas as she rode past him, seeing the amusement in his eyes. Did he find this funny?

She frowned. He probably did.

But it didn't matter. She and Freckles were going on a ride and didn't plan to return for hours. Hopefully by then, Lucas would have concluded his business at the house.

Yes, she was avoiding him. She didn't bother denying it. She needed time to organize her thoughts. Abby still had no idea what to do about that kiss.

She raced down the road, leaving Lucas and the house behind in a cloud of dust. After about a mile, she slowed Freckles' pace, rubbing the horse's neck briskly. "Thank you for rescuing me, girl."

Abby's muscles slowly relaxed, but she didn't feel at peace. The kiss between her and Lucas bothered her. But the longer she thought about it, the more she realized it wasn't because she regretted it. It was because it reminded her what she was missing in her life.

She'd kissed other men, and while pleasant, none of those short embraces compared, even for a second, to what it had been like in Lucas' arms.

What was she going to do? She didn't know if she could stay at the house, knowing Lucas could show up at any time. She scrubbed a hand over her face. This was all such a mess.

As she rode down the road in silence, contemplating her options, she heard a soft thundering, and realized someone was coming up behind her. It wasn't often she passed others on the road, but it wasn't unheard of.

She moved over to the side, allowing plenty of room for the rider to pass.

But as the sound grew closer, the horse's strides slowed. Finally, she glanced over her shoulder, jumping when Lucas moved his horse next to hers.

Aghast, she shook her head. "What are you doing here? I thought you were meeting with Charlotte about the shop?"

He rested his reins over the saddle horn. "I was. But I also wanted to speak with you. You've been avoiding me."

She shook her head automatically. "I have not." The lie was ridiculous even to her own ears. Finally, she nodded slowly. "I'm sorry."

"Why?" He waited for her eyes to meet his. "Do you regret what happened?"

It was a tough question, one she'd asked herself repeatedly. "I don't. At least, I don't blame you, or myself. Frankly, it was bound to happen eventually." She offered him a weak smile, but he didn't look satisfied.

He nodded slowly. "True, from the moment I saw you, I wanted that to happen. But more than anything, I want you to be all right. I don't want to do anything you'll regret."

"Thank you," she said softly. She could tell he meant it, and she trusted him. Lucas never lied. "I truly don't regret it. I just don't know what I'm supposed to do now."

His leg brushed against hers companionably. "Do you have to do anything?"

"I feel like I need to. This isn't easy. It's messy, confusing, and I'm not sure how I feel about it."

"I meant what I said the other day. I want us to at least be friends, if at all possible. But if you decide you want nothing to do with me, I'll accept that. This time, the choice is yours."

She appreciated what he was saying, but that's what made it even more difficult. This time, it *was* her choice. If she continued to see him, to become friends with him again, and her heart was crushed, it would be her fault. She'd have no one to blame but herself.

But more than anything, she didn't want to live her life in fear. She was afraid of getting close to Lucas because she feared the pain that could follow. But what kind of life was that? She shook her head softly. "That almost makes it harder."

He nodded knowingly. "I know. But it's what you deserve."

She let out a slow breath and stopped her horse. She dismounted, needing to think. Lucas followed her lead and dropped to the ground, petting his horse one last time before it started grazing with Freckles.

She walked a few feet before turning around and walking back, trampling the grass beneath her boots. "I can't deny there's still a spark between us, but sharing such intimacy isn't something friends do."

He rocked back on his heels. "No. At least I'd hope not."

She held up her hands. "Exactly. So if we're not friends, then what are we doing?"

"Courting?"

She shook her head firmly. "No. That's not possible."

He came to her then and took her hands in his. "Why not?"

"Why not?" She didn't try to hide her astonishment. "Because of what happened in the past. Because of Rhys. Because of me, you, everything. It's not that simple."

"It could be. If Rhys knew this is what you wanted, he'd allow it."

"It's not about if he would allow it or not. I'm older now and in possession of my fortune. Rhys has no say, but I still don't want him to worry. And if I explored a relationship with you, after all that has happened, he *would* worry." She bit her lip. "Besides, I'm not sure it's the best thing for me. Several men are already courting me, and I'm not comfortable telling them I'm unavailable."

A flash entered his eyes, and he hid it quickly, but it was enough to see he was jealous. "I won't stop others from courting you, but I want to see where this goes. I want to explore if there's anything still between us."

He didn't push her, didn't try to persuade her further. Just remained silent, allowing her to think over everything, while holding her hands. She tried to rationalize away her feelings for him, to tell herself it was only physical, that she could find that with someone else, but she couldn't manage it.

The truth was, she'd never forgotten Lucas. She'd never stopped wanting him. That was why she'd run away when her family told her it was time to marry. She could've settled down with someone, been content, had a family, but it wasn't what she wanted. Deep down, even though she told herself she'd moved on, all she wanted was Lucas.

But now that he was standing in front of her, offering her that dream, she was afraid to move forward. Afraid of being hurt.

She closed her eyes and took a deep breath before looking at him. "I would like to see what this is, to see if it's anything more than an echo from the past." He was about to say something, but she reached up and placed a finger over his lips. "But if we're going to do this, Rhys can't know. Then if things don't work out, it won't matter, and he won't worry."

"But if they do?"

"If we fall in love and decide to have a future together, we'll tell him."

His chest rose and fell a little quicker with each breath. "Are you sure?"

She nodded slowly, forcing herself to act sensibly. "I am. As long as we're discreet, we can explore what's here."

At her words, he wrapped his arm around her waist and slowly pulled her close. "And what exactly does *exploring* entail?"

Goosebumps rose on her arms at his touch, at the soft words he spoke. "It includes talking, spending time with one another. Kissing," she added, finally brave enough.

He looked pleased. "Ah. And where shall we start?" He wrapped his other arm around her and slowly moved his hands up and down her back.

She leaned into his touch, fighting back a moan at how good it felt. "That isn't fair," she said, her voice breathless.

He leaned forward, feathered a kiss at her neck, and whispered, "What isn't?"

"This. What you're doing. How you make me feel."

"Oh, this is plenty fair. Because everything you feel is what's inside me too."

Her eyes closed slowly, his words echoing through her mind. It seemed like the years fell away and it was just the two of them again, in love. But she needed to remember that's not what this was. They weren't in love. It wasn't eight years ago. It was now, and things were different.

He didn't try to kiss her, just held her and occasionally nuzzled her neck, but it sent sparks throughout her body.

He pulled back then and looked into her eyes. "When can I see you again?"

It took her a moment to clear the haze he'd woven over her mind. She frowned slightly. "I'm not sure."

"Next week, I'm hosting a hiring fair for the mine. It's mainly business, but there'll be food and some games. I've also invited the other women. Would you come?"

A smile bloomed on her lips. "Yes. I'd definitely like to

come. Although, we won't be alone." She wondered how he would react to her statement, but he only smiled.

"I wouldn't imagine otherwise. But, since we're not going to be alone then, we better make the most of it now." A devilish glint lit his eyes.

She bit her lip, playing along. "Whatever do you mean?"

He shrugged playfully. "Well, this seems like our last opportunity."

"Opportunity for what?" Her voice sounded breathy.

He leaned forward slightly, his lips hovering above hers. "To show you how much I'm going to miss this." His lips met hers then, and all joking fell away.

Their last kiss had been shocking, strong, and in a way, desperate. Now they had all the time in the world, and Lucas was drawing out every second.

He kissed her once, twice, then nipped her bottom lip, sucking it into his mouth. She gasped. She'd always loved it when he did that.

"I love the way you respond to me." His whisper was guttural, as if it was taking everything in him to hold back.

"I love the way you kiss me," she admitted.

He groaned, lifting his hands to cradle her head, before fitting his mouth to hers.

This was coming home. And as she fell into the web he wove around her, she couldn't have been happier. For the first time in years, she felt hope.

CHAPTER 12

Lucas shook another man's hand and nodded politely in greeting before glancing around the rest of the crowd. The job fair was in full swing in the field by the church, and at least two hundred men had shown up. It wouldn't provide all the labor they'd need, but it was a good start.

Lucas excelled in instantly knowing whether someone was a good hire or not. It was another reason he'd been sent here ahead of the others.

The man in front of him held his gaze, and Lucas already knew this man would do well for their operation. He was thin, almost to the point of being gaunt, but there was a glint in his eyes that showed he was hungry, both for food and for success. His coat was thin, and it looked like the sleeves had been patched several times, but he didn't seem self-conscious.

"You're hired," Lucas said, making the decision on the spot.

The man's surprised expression quickly turned into a grin, and he shook Lucas' hand harder. "You won't regret it."

"I know. You'll do well here. Unlike other operations, you

can make a name for yourself with us. Do well in the mine, and you can move up."

The man paused, taking in Lucas' words. "Thank you," he said a little more reverently.

Lucas nodded. "Go on and enjoy yourself. There won't be much time for such things once the work starts."

The man didn't have to be told twice, and he left with a final nod of thanks.

Lucas looked around again for what felt like the hundredth time, but he still didn't see Abby. He knew she'd come, she always kept her word. Besides, the other women were supposed to be here as well, and they likely would drive together. She'd be here.

It was then the realization hit him.

He was *nervous*.

It surprised him. He hadn't felt this way—giddy, nervous, excited—in eight years.

Just those feelings alone showed him he'd made the right choice. What he wanted with Abby was much deeper than friendship.

He glanced over his shoulder again just as the ladies parked their wagon, and his gaze searched her out. She'd been watching the crowd, but almost as if she felt him watching her, she turned to look at him. A slow smile came to her lips, but other than that, she didn't acknowledge him.

He wanted to go to her then, to take her into his arms, but he couldn't. She'd set firm boundaries, and he would respect them.

No matter how much he wanted otherwise.

He discreetly watched her as she mingled with the crowd, laughing with other men, greeting some of the women who'd shown up. It was overwhelming how much he wanted to be by her side, to hear what she had to say about the gathering, about the potential employees.

In truth, he wanted to spend every moment with her. Things had gotten complicated quickly. But again, he didn't mind that. In fact, he wished things would speed up between them, no matter how much confusion it caused.

Another man hailed her from across the field, snagging Lucas' attention as well. He maintained the conversation he was having with another potential worker, already knowing the man wouldn't be a good fit. Only half listening, Lucas watched the interaction between Abby and the gentleman she spoke with.

Looking more closely, Lucas realized it was the gentleman he'd been standing next to at the quick courting soiree at the hotel. The one who'd said he was pursuing Abby.

New feelings rose within him, ones he wasn't proud of but didn't bother denying. He was jealous, and he didn't like it one bit that she was speaking with another suitor.

He nodded at the potential worker he spoke with, cutting him off mid-sentence. "Thank you for your interest, we'll be in touch to let you know if you have the job."

The man realized he wouldn't be hired, but instead of arguing, he nodded and accepted the decision gracefully. His reaction almost swayed Lucas, but with the mining activity in the area, the man would find another job quickly.

Lucas walked past another group of potential employees, no doubt waiting to speak with him, and made his way over to Abby.

They *were* acquaintances after all. It was perfectly acceptable to greet her.

Abby glanced over her shoulder, her eyes widening at his approach, but he didn't turn around. He walked up to the couple, nodding politely. "Good afternoon, Miss Winthrop, Sir. I hope you're enjoying yourselves."

The man grinned broadly and shook Lucas' hand. "Good to see you again. I didn't introduce myself when we met. I'm

Connor Broderick." He nodded toward the gathering. "This is a great way to recruit. It's convinced me to do something similar when I expand my own operation."

"We found it's the best way to get good help quickly." Lucas glanced around at the crowd. "This isn't anywhere near enough manpower, but it's a start."

Lucas turned to Abby. "I hope it was an easy drive."

"It was. No more ambushes." She chuckled.

Connor shook his head, a frown appearing on his face. "I heard about that. Glad you're all safe." He glanced over Abby's shoulder at the other women she'd arrived with. "It looks like they're adjusting well. I heard one of them will open a shop soon." He looked at Lucas. "Is that true?"

Lucas nodded. "Miss Hayer is opening a bakery."

The man smiled broadly. "A bakery? An excellent addition to town. Don't get me wrong, I like Sally's just fine, but I have a feeling a bakery will do quite well."

Lucas nodded. People in town were desperate for another place to dine, and he had no doubts Miss Hayer's establishment would thrive.

"Charlotte is so excited," Abby added. "She can't stop talking about it."

"All we need to do is find the right place," Lucas agreed.

Connor tilted his head. "I might know of a place. It isn't available yet, but I think it might be soon. I'll need to check on it, but if you'd like, I could inform you once I know."

Lucas' brows rose. "I'd appreciate that. Thank you."

The man nodded agreeably and then looked back to Abby, dismissing Lucas. The awkwardness grew, and Abby glanced at Lucas, silently nudging him along. His lips quirked. "I apologize if I interrupted something important."

The man looked at him, not nearly as friendly as he'd been before. His eyes narrowed slightly. "You were, in fact, interrupting. But we don't mind, do we, Abby?"

Lucas gritted his teeth at the familiar way the man spoke to her. Everything in him ached to correct him, to demand he refer to her as Miss Winthrop.

Abby smiled, but the corners looked tight. "No. Of course not. Mr. McDermott is always welcome."

"Yes..." Connor drew the word out, but then smiled and gave Abby his full attention. "In any case, I wanted to speak with you to see if you'd allow me to drive you home."

Abby's head pulled back slightly, surprised. "Oh. Yes, I'd like that. Thank you, Mr. Broderick."

Connor lit up, his grin triumphant. He didn't look in Lucas' direction to rub it in, but Lucas felt his elation all the same.

"It's my pleasure. Take your time, and enjoy yourself. I'm in no rush to leave."

She bowed her head slightly. "You're too kind."

Connor smiled before leaving with a little bounce in his step.

Abby cleared her throat, and then looked at Lucas. "How are you?"

"I'm doing well. Truly though, I am glad to see you made it all right." He spoke easily, like the conversation only moments before hadn't taken place. He wasn't going to comment on Connor—that was her choice, and he meant to respect it.

Her shoulders relaxed. "I'm relieved as well. I'll probably think of that mob for some time while coming into town."

"I don't blame you." He smiled slowly. "So, I was hoping to steal you away. I would have offered to drive you home, but it appears I'm too late."

Her lips quirked in amusement. "Yes. I'm not sure what happened just now."

"He marked you."

"What do you mean?"

He leaned a little closer, unable to help himself. "He was staking his claim. He wanted me to know you're with him."

As expected, her mouth fell open. "I don't belong to anyone!" she whispered her outrage. She huffed. "But you're right. That's what he was doing." She shook her head. "The men here, they're so aggressive."

"They need to be, with so few women." Lucas could see she didn't like how the men could be, but she didn't blame them. She understood all too well. Still, he didn't care how desperate the men were, Lucas wanted to keep her all to himself.

He reached out and brushed a fingertip over her sleeve. Her eyes darted to the side in case someone watched them, but Lucas angled himself so no one saw the caress. "Can I see you tonight? I can find something to talk about with the others if we need an excuse."

She bit her lip then finally nodded. "I want that too."

That one little admission was all it took to set him at ease. She wanted to spend time with him. It was a start. And his heart swelled. "Then I'll be there."

She gave him a small, secret smile. "I look forward to it, *Mr. McDermott*," she said his name a little louder, a devilish glint in her eye.

He took her hand, bending low, and placed a lingering kiss over it. "Miss Winthrop."

She allowed him to hold her hand a moment longer before she extricated it and headed off, leaving him to watch her saunter away.

It was a view he would never tire of.

CHAPTER 13

Abby sat quietly in the front of the carriage as Connor chatted amiably next to her. He was a good man. Kind, thoughtful, and she'd been grateful to have his attention the last several months.

But right now, her thoughts weren't on him, they were on the man she knew was waiting at the house for her.

She'd lingered at the job fair until the end, telling the other women to ride on ahead without her. Lucas had nodded at her from across the field, reconfirming their meeting, but she hadn't needed the reassurance.

She knew Lucas would be there.

Connor said something, drawing her attention. "Pardon?" she asked, feeling guilty for her inattention.

He glanced at her with an indulgent smile. "I said, thank you again for allowing me to drive you home."

"Oh. It's most appreciated." She smiled tightly at him, hoping he wouldn't see how much she looked forward to its end.

They were about to round the last bend to the house, when he stopped the carriage and turned toward her. The movement rang an alarm bell within her. "Is everything all right?" she asked.

He nodded slowly then took her hands in his. She swallowed hard, already knowing what he would say.

He looked into her eyes. "Abby, I hope you know how much it's meant to me to get to know you over the last few months. And I hope you've enjoyed getting to know me as well."

He seemed to want a response, so she nodded, unable to speak through the lump in her throat.

"Good." He rubbed his thumb over her hand. "I wanted you alone because there's something in particular I wanted to ask you. I think you might have some idea."

She shook her head quickly, hoping to forestall the conversation.

He just laughed. "I love how modest and demure you are. I find it very becoming in a woman."

If he truly thought she was modest and demure, he didn't know her well. He'd courted her, but they'd never really gotten past pleasantries. "Mr. Broderick—"

"Connor, please. Abby, I think you know I care for you. I've come to think of you as the most delicate, gentle, intelligent woman of my acquaintance. I admire you greatly. And I hope my feelings are reciprocated. I haven't spoken with your brother, because I wanted to speak with you first, to give you the choice, but I'm hoping you'll do me the honor of marrying me."

"Connor—"

He shook his head firmly. "No. Please don't answer now. I know this is sooner than expected, and I would like for you to have time to properly consider it. I'm in no rush, but I could no longer go on without telling you my intentions. Please, tell me you'll consider it."

Abby was uncertain what to say. She wanted to say no, but

was that the right thing? Connor was a good man, and he would make a wonderful husband. She didn't love him, but was that really the most important thing in a marriage? She'd be a fool to turn him down immediately. So she nodded. "I'll think about it."

He squeezed her hand and grinned. "Thank you. That's all I can ask for."

Knowing he shouldn't push his luck for more, he picked up the reins and set the horses walking.

They didn't speak again until they got to the house. He descended from the carriage, rounded it, and helped her down. He held her an extra moment before releasing her, and the contact was uncomfortable for Abby. Not necessarily unpleasant, but she wondered if Lucas was there, watching their interaction.

For some reason, it felt wrong to touch Connor any more than necessary.

She took a step back, smiling broadly to cover her discomfort. "Thank you again for the ride home."

"It was my pleasure. And please, take your time considering what I said."

"I will. I promise. Thank you again, Connor."

He reached out and brushed his thumb over her jaw like he wanted to pull her in for a kiss, but she kept her stance rigid, showing in every way that such contact wasn't welcome.

Sensing it, he smiled and nodded at her again, dropping his hand. "Good night."

"Good night," she said as he climbed up into the carriage and rode away.

She stayed outside for a few moments, watching him drive down the road. The sun lowered over the hills, and while it was warm, a chill washed through her. She scrubbed her arms quickly, hoping to ease it, but she felt unsettled.

Why had a proposal from a man who'd been courting her

for six months make her feel uneasy, unsettled, hollow. She should be overjoyed.

But instead, she felt like a bag of rocks sat in her stomach.

A throat cleared behind her, and she spun around, spotting Lucas in the doorway. She swallowed hard. "How long have you been standing there?"

"I just opened the door." He stepped out and closed the door behind him. "Is everything all right?" His tone turned grim. "Did something happen?"

The urge to tell him about the proposal, to confide in him, was overwhelming. But she didn't give in to the impulse. As much as she felt a connection with Lucas, Abby didn't know exactly where they stood. "Everything is fine. I'm just tired," she said lamely. "It's been a long day."

He took a few more steps toward her but didn't reach out and touch her. "Do you want to go inside?"

"No. Not yet." She heaved a heavy breath. "Physically I'm tired, but my mind is racing."

"How about a walk?"

She glanced up at the sky. "It'll be dark soon."

He reached forward to take her hand, but gave her sufficient time to reject the gesture. "We'll stay close to the house."

No matter how tired she was, the thought of having Lucas to herself, was too much to resist. She squeezed his hand. "All right."

He gave her a big smile, and it filled her with warmth. How did he affect her like that? Just being near him, being with him, filled her with longing, with butterflies, and a myriad of other sensations. She was attracted to him, but it was more than that. A part of her still loved him, no matter what had happened, no matter how long it had been.

The real question was did she love the Lucas from back then—the memories—or did she love him now?

If only it were that easy. The past and the present blurred, and it was impossible to separate them.

He placed her hand on his arm, tucking her in next to him. "Are you warm enough?"

"Yes." She tilted her face up to the sky and took a deep breath. "We'll blink, and there'll be piles of snow everywhere. I want to enjoy this weather as long as possible."

"Anything you want."

Her heart trembled. *Anything you want*. He offered it just as he had in the past. He used to say he would give her anything she wanted, that he would fill her life with happiness, that she'd want for nothing.

And then he'd left.

"What is it?" he asked, and she realized she'd stiffened up.

When she didn't respond right away, he stopped, gently turning her toward him. He placed both his hands along her jaw, tilting her face up, so he could look at her. The last light of day reflected in his eyes, and she felt the ache spread.

"This is hard," she whispered.

"What is?"

"This. Us." She tapped her finger against his chest, then hers. "I don't know what to do."

"What do you want to do?"

If only it were that easy. She shook her head slowly. "I don't want to get hurt."

"I'll do everything in my power to keep that from happening. You can trust me."

His words were said easily, and she knew he meant them. At least for now. But what would happen in the future? What would happen tomorrow, next week, next month, or two years from now? That's what she was worried about. That's what concerned her. When Lucas' job was finished here, what then? Would he go back to the East? "I want to trust you." She finally said what was in her heart. "But I'm afraid."

He nodded slowly, understanding. "I know. And it's going to take time. I broke your trust, and that's a hard thing to come back from. But as each day passes, as you see how things are now, it will slowly come back." He placed a soft kiss against her lips, and she shivered at the contact.

"I feel so confused."

"I know. I'm sorry. Is there anything I can do to reassure you?"

She thought it over seriously. What more could he do? He was attentive, kind, was clearly expressing what he wanted. But none of those things healed old wounds. "Keep doing what you're doing. It'll just take me some time."

They finished their walk back in silence, thoughts churning through her mind.

When they returned to the house, he stopped before opening the door. She looked at him expectantly, but he remained silent, looking contemplative.

Finally, he met her gaze. "I know you're worried, and you have every right to be. I know I broke your trust, and I'm sorry. If I need to, I'll say that for the rest of my life. I'm sorry for what happened between us."

She placed a finger over his lips, feeling the soft skin. "You don't need to apologize again."

With her finger still on his lips, he reached up and wrapped his fingers around her wrist, holding her there. Without saying a word, he moved her arm to the side and slowly pulled her forward until he could wrap his other arm around her waist. It was like they were about to dance a waltz, but they weren't swaying to music. The only things moving were the trees, dancing in the wind.

"I don't want to pressure you. I want to give you all the time in the world to figure out how you feel about me and what you want out of life. But there's something I need to tell you."

Her heart beat heavily in her chest. "What?"

He pulled her in closer, resting his forehead against hers. "I want to be with you. I want everyone to know we're together, that we care for one another. I don't want you to see other men, to be courted by anyone but me. I want the chance to win you over, to gain that trust back. I left because I wasn't worthy of you, at least, I didn't feel I was. But that was about our stations, about money, about supporting you. I've always been your equal in heart. And seeing you again, being with you, has shown me that again."

She reeled, and before she could respond, he shook his head, silencing her. "I want you with me, Abby. But this time, it doesn't matter what I want. It matters what *you* want, what you need. Whatever you desire, I'll do it. Whether that's to be with you and never leave your side...or to leave. This choice is yours. But if you're not ready, if you need more time, you have it."

She didn't know what to say, how to respond. Her initial reaction was to wrap her arms around his neck, kiss him, and tell him she loved him and never wanted to part from him. But she wasn't certain. Were these feelings real? She still didn't know. And without knowing, she couldn't say those things—it wouldn't be fair, to either of them.

As silence remained, he squeezed her tightly. "You don't need to answer now."

"Thank you. I'm just not ready."

He pulled back from her, looking her in the eye, and nodded. "I understand. This isn't an ultimatum. I'm not leaving anytime soon. I don't want to pressure you for anything you're not ready to give. I just want you to know how I feel." His eyes settled on her lips. "May I kiss you?"

Her heart melted at the request, and everything in her ached for his touch. "Yes. Yes, please." She wrapped her arms around his shoulders to pull him close.

Slowly, almost achingly, he lowered his lips to hers. The first brush sent shockwaves through her, tingling down to her fingertips, her toes, and back up. Her heart fluttered like crazy, the feeling echoing in her stomach. She was a mess, a glorious, nerve-filled mess. And she'd never felt like this with anyone. That had to mean *something*.

She was still trying to figure out what it all meant when he pulled away, placing one last kiss on her lips before letting go. "I'll see you soon."

"All right. Goodnight."

As he walked away, he glanced over his shoulder, sending her another smile. He didn't push her for commitments, didn't pressure her. Instead, he left it completely in her hands.

She still wasn't sure if she loved the Lucas from then or now. What she *did* know was that the present Lucas was dangerous to her heart.

CHAPTER 14

Before Lucas mounted his horse, Abby stepped inside, closed the door, and leaned against it. She didn't want to watch him ride away. She was worried she might call him back and promise things she wasn't ready for.

How had this happened? Wasn't it just a week ago they'd decided to be friends? Things had gotten serious so quickly, it boggled the mind.

She was wrung out, exhausted. Especially after her drive home with Connor and then her time with Lucas. She scrubbed a hand over her face. She still had no idea what to do.

She couldn't give Lucas the exclusivity he wanted. She couldn't give up her life, everything she'd built, now that he wanted a life with her. Doing so would be foolish, and she'd made an effort over the years to never be foolish again.

And now Connor had proposed. She closed her eyes and whimpered.

"Is everything all right?" Lily's voice was wry with amusement.

Abby opened her eyes and grimaced. "I'm not sure, but I hope it will be. Someday."

Lily turned a bit more serious. "The others and I would like to talk to you."

Abby's stomach dropped. "That doesn't sound good."

"It isn't bad."

Abby sensed Lily's hedging. "But?"

"Hannah saw you outside with Lucas." Lily sent her a sympathetic smile. "Suffice it to say, everyone knows there's something between you two."

Abby groaned.

Lily took a step forward. "Look, I know it's none of our business. And really, you don't need to tell us anything you don't want to. I think everyone is just concerned." She shrugged, and a small smile quirked her lips. "And maybe we just want some juicy gossip."

Abby laughed and pushed herself away from the door. "Well then, I might as well tell you guys everything."

"You *did* say it was a long story. We have the whole night ahead of us."

"That's true." Her voice echoed her reluctance.

Lily nodded toward the back of the house, where the kitchen was. "Come on. Charlotte even has a cake for us."

"I guess that makes it all better," she grumbled.

As they walked toward the kitchen, Abby wanted to turn and run away. How was she supposed to talk about what had happened or how she felt, when she had no idea about either? It was like her life was a runaway horse and she was standing on the sidelines, watching it bolt toward the hills. She wasn't in charge. She wasn't in control. How was she supposed to make sense of any of this?

As Lily and Abby stepped into the kitchen, all chatter ceased, and everyone looked over at Abby. Lily joined the group, but Abby stood there like an outsider. She shifted on her feet. "So, I guess you all want to hear the story now."

Charlotte and Grace smiled, and Hannah's eyebrows rose. Emery shrugged and said, "Only if you want to share it with us. Truly, it's none of our business." She glared at the others.

Charlotte turned and grabbed a thickly frosted cake from the counter behind her. "I have something to break the ice."

Grace rubbed her hands together. "Finally. That cake has tortured me all day."

Some of the others laughed, but not Hannah. She didn't look angry or upset. Just...emotionless. It unnerved her to see such a mask outside of the upper circles. People in town responded freely, naturally, and Abby was never left wondering what they thought or how they felt. She knew Hannah had her eyes set on Lucas, but did she truly care for him, or was she only after his fortune?

Charlotte made quick work of cutting the cake and handing slices to everyone. And after just one bite, with sugar coating her taste buds, she felt a little better. "This cake is magic," she finally said into the silence as the others enjoyed their pieces as well.

Lily tipped her fork toward Abby. "I was just thinking that. Very well done, Charlotte."

Charlotte bubbled with the praise. She was obviously happy to have brought joy to each of them through her food. "I'm happy to teach any of you how to make this."

Licking her fork, Grace shook her head. "I'd rather just eat it after you make it."

Hannah raised an eyebrow, daintily setting her fork down once her piece was finished. "What are you going to do when she leaves to open her shop?"

"I'll go to town every day and buy one," she said, matter-of-factly.

Hannah nodded as if it were the most logical thing to do.

"Good idea." She pushed the plate away from her and looked to Abby now that everyone had finished. "Why don't you tell us what's between you and Lucas, Abby."

"Only if you want to," Emery stressed one more time.

Absentmindedly, Abby toyed with her fork. "I didn't mean to deceive anyone. There's just a lot I haven't figured out."

Lily placed her hand on Abby's forearm. "No one here thought you were being dishonest." She looked at the others. "Right?"

Everyone murmured their agreement. Even Hannah, although Abby wasn't so sure she meant it.

Abby finally put her fork down and leaned against the counter. "There's still so much I don't know how to explain."

"Why not start from the beginning?" Charlotte offered a small smile.

So for the next half hour, Abby poured her heart out, hoping and praying they would understand, that they wouldn't pass judgment. She didn't go into details about the intimacies she'd shared with Lucas, but they knew enough to understand they'd been madly in love.

When she was done explaining their history, everyone was silent, flabbergasted.

"So..." Hannah was obviously trying to wrap her mind around what had happened. "You hadn't heard or seen from Mr. McDermott since he left you eight years ago? Seeing him at the train platform was the first time?"

Abby bit her lip, nodding. "Yes. I was shocked. I had no idea he was one of the Copper Kings or that I would see him that day."

Emery just shook her head in disbelief. "I'm so sorry. No wonder you seemed bewildered."

"Anyone would be," Grace added.

Hannah held up her hand. "So, are you involved with him again? I'm assuming so from what I saw out the window."

Abby flushed, and both Emery and Lily scolded Hannah.

Before they could really tear into her, Abby held up her hands. "No. It's a fair question. We've decided to explore how we feel about each other. But not openly. I think you can all understand why I wouldn't want to tell my brother about this."

For a moment, Abby worried Hannah would do just that if she were upset enough. But when all of them nodded, including Hannah, Abby knew it would be all right. "Thank you."

Grace cocked her head. "So, while you're figuring out your relationship with Mr. McDermott, what about your other suitors? What about Mr. Broderick?"

"Ah. W—well," she stammered, "they're still courting me."

Hannah's brows rose. "What does Mr. McDermott think about that?"

"He knows. He'd prefer otherwise, but he doesn't have a choice in the matter." Her chin raised a notch, and Charlotte and Grace shared a look.

Lily rubbed a finger on the countertop. "I see."

Abby could feel the weight of their speculation, their judgments, and it exhausted her. She buried her face in her hands. "I know this is complicated. Trust me, I wish this wasn't happening." Before anyone could say anything, she threw her head back up. She was done being quiet—she needed to speak her mind. "I mean, what am I supposed to do here? How is this supposed to work out? It ended horribly before—I almost didn't make it. So what am I doing now?"

No one answered for a moment, then finally, Emery smiled. "You're trying to find happiness. Same as us. I find that when something's uncomfortable—when it's hard, when you're really being tested—that's when change happens. When *miracles* happen. You're going to come out of this, and no matter what, you're going to be fine. More than that, you're going to *thrive*."

The others nodded their agreement, and with their support, her heart lightened. "You really think so?"

"I do. Just do what feels right to you. Don't let anyone persuade you otherwise."

Abby smiled. "Thank you. All of you. I was concerned over how this conversation would end, but you've all made me feel so much better."

Charlotte smiled smugly. "My cakes have that effect on people."

There was a slight pause, then everyone burst into laughter, including Charlotte.

Abby's stomach hurt by the time she stopped laughing, and she looked at each of the women in turn, their eyes filled with merriment. They were starting to become like sisters, starting to *matter* to one another, and that meant more than she could ever say.

Looking at Charlotte, Abby leaned forward. "Do you have any more cake?"

"Oh, I *always* have cake."

CHAPTER 15

D*o what feels right*, Abby told herself for what felt like the hundredth time. *Do what feels right.*

She blew out a deep breath as she rode into town. The cookies she'd helped bake were wrapped and securely tucked in her saddlebags.

The others weren't riding into town with her today, but after going almost a week without seeing Lucas, she decided she needed to make the effort to spend time with him.

He'd been trapped in the mining office in town all week, interviewing and hiring for the operation. He must be exhausted.

Exhausted and hungry.

At least she hoped so. Though she guessed the cookies would be well received either way. She smiled softly. He'd always had a sweet tooth.

She waved to a few men as they passed by, and discreetly scanned the streets for her brother or Willow. With them conveniently out of sight, she dismounted in front of Lucas' office, relieved to see a man just leaving the building. With any luck, she'd find him alone.

She quickly grabbed the cookies out of her bag, unwrapped the cloth tied around the basket, and slipped inside the building. Glancing one last time over her shoulder, she smiled, pleased she'd escaped Rhys' notice.

She didn't enjoy deceiving her brother, but in a way, it made her relationship with Lucas a little more exciting.

As she closed the door behind her, Lucas continued writing, scribbling on a piece of paper. "I'll be with you in just a moment."

He hadn't even glanced up. Abby felt as an amused smile creep onto her lips. "Take your time."

At her voice, his head snapped up, and his smile crinkled his eyes. "What are you doing here?"

He got up from his chair, came around the desk, and took her hands in his. She felt giddy. "Well, I haven't seen you in a while. I thought I should check and make sure you're still alive."

"Sorry. I've been busy." He ran his hand through his disheveled hair and the strands stood on end. The top button on his collar was undone, and his shirtsleeves were rolled up. His hand was stained with ink and lead, like he'd been scribbling nonstop for days. He probably had.

She raised a brow at him. "Maybe I should have come sooner. Have you been sleeping? Eating?"

He shrugged. "Here and there."

She sighed dramatically. "Well, I guess it's good I brought these, then." She pulled her basket of treats from behind her and offered them to him.

He groaned in gratitude as he took them from her. "You remembered."

"Remembered?" She pretended to not know what he was talking about.

"That these are my favorite."

"Some things you never forget."

"Well, that's true." He laughed, snatching one of the cookies and taking a big bite. His eyes closed. "You're a goddess."

"They're all for you," she said with amusement. "You can eat as many as you want."

"Thank you." He took another bite before placing the basket on his desk. "Do you want to sit?"

She glanced back at the door. "Are you sure? Do you have time?"

"I always have time for you."

The words, spoken so easily, made her heart flutter. "Then I'll have a seat," she said, sitting in a chair right in front of him. She had to tilt her head back to look at him, but once he leaned against the desk, it wasn't too bad.

He crossed his legs while munching on another cookie. "How have you been?"

She didn't really want to talk about the turmoil she was feeling, the confusion over him and Connor, so instead she said, "Fine. Just keeping busy. I've been finishing up a dress order for Willow."

The cookie paused halfway to his mouth. "Dress order?"

She could see his confusion. She chuckled. "I work for Willow. She owns a dress business, and I do some of the extra work for her.

"You have a job. You *work*," he said, as if trying to wrap his brain around the notion. "But what about your inheritance?" His eyes slitted. "Is Rhys withholding it?"

She laughed, amused he couldn't believe she'd work willingly. "No. I'm in possession of my fortune. I just also happen to work for Willow."

"Why?"

"Why not?" She lifted her hands. "I have plenty of time.

Anyway, what would I do otherwise? Sit and drink tea all day?" She rolled her eyes.

"It's what a lot of women in your station do."

She shrugged. "I'm not like the other women of our station, I guess."

"No. You aren't." Before she could decide how she felt about his statement, he added, "But I like that about you."

Warmth filled her as she saw the appreciation in his eyes. He respected her choice, and that filled her with satisfaction.

"What about after you marry? Will you continue working?"

She nodded slowly, thinking it over. "I'd like to. It all depends on my husband's job and what my other duties are. At least in the beginning, before any children come, I'd assume so." She blushed. Speaking of her hypothetical children, *their* children, embarrassed her.

He smiled, a gleam entering his eyes like he was imagining their life together. "I think whatever you choose, your husband will support you."

"I hope so. Otherwise, he's not the kind of man I want to marry."

He shook his head. "If he doesn't support you, he's not worthy of you."

She looked at him, and although he didn't say the words, she knew what he meant. *He* would support her. *He* would allow her to choose whatever she wanted. That meant a lot to her. "Thank you."

He nodded then took another bite of his cookie. "I'm glad you came in today."

She bit her lip. "I couldn't let you starve to death, could I?"

"I guess not."

"Will you work late again tonight?" She didn't want to ask him to come spend time with her if he was busy.

He let out a long breath and looked at the ceiling. "I sure hope not. I've gotten most of the initial hiring done, and that was the main work I needed to do. "

"That's good, right?"

He nodded. "Yes. We have about one hundred and fifty workers now."

The number surprised her. "So many?"

"It's a large operation."

She clucked her tongue. "I'll say."

He finished his cookie and brushed off his hands, but instead of reaching for another, he took her hands in his. Warmth enveloped her fingers, and she felt content just having the connection. "Do you want me to come by tonight?"

She loved that he gave her the choice. "Yes. I've missed you," she said softly.

He tugged her hand, pulling her up from her chair, and she freely stepped into his arms. "I've missed you too."

She didn't know how it was possible to feel both at ease and on edge at the same time. "It's been hard, staying away from you."

"You don't *need* to stay away from me."

"But you've had work to do."

He shrugged. "Nothing is as important as you. You can interrupt me anytime you want. You will always have my attention when you need it."

What he was offering her, to put her first, was more than anyone had ever done. "Are you sure?"

He used to feel very differently. Success had always been more important than their relationship in the past.

He nodded slowly then tilted her chin up so her eyes met his. "I promise nothing will ever come ahead of you again." He brushed his lips softly across hers, sealing his words.

When he finally released her, she sucked in a deep breath to steady herself. "I better go."

He nodded and reluctantly released her.

She smoothed her skirts, smiling at him. "I'll see you tonight."

"I can't wait."

The way he looked at her, the way he watched her, greedily devouring her with his eyes, told her how much he truly meant that.

And as she walked out the door, she realized she'd never looked forward to an evening more.

◈

AFTER A WEEK OF LUCAS VISITING HER IN THE EVENINGS and Abby sneaking into his office during the day, she'd come to a solid conclusion—she was in love with him.

She couldn't pinpoint exactly when the realization hit, but when she dismounted in front of his office again, she knew.

And she wanted to tell him she loved him—that she wanted to be with him and *only* him—today. She was certain Connor would be disappointed when she refused him, but he would move on.

She smiled, just thinking of Lucas' reaction. He'd been patient with her, allowing her to figure her feelings out on her own, never giving her grief when another man asked to drive her home or to take a walk with her.

He hadn't liked those things, but he'd given her the choice. And because of that, she loved him.

The past and the present intermingled, her love for him back then and now joined together to make her feelings stronger, richer. She saw that now, even though they'd gone through hardships, instead of damaging the relationship, their past only made it stronger.

She twisted her hands in front of her, wringing them with excited nerves. She darted a few glances around to make sure no one saw her enter the office, but it was halfhearted.

She'd realized Rhys and Willow were busy this time of day with the hotel, so they weren't likely to discover her.

Taking a deep breath, she gripped the doorknob and pulled it open.

Immediately, Lucas glanced up, pushed away from his desk, and came to her. He picked her up, twirled her around, and placed a warm kiss on her lips. "You need to start coming in earlier."

She laughed as he set her down. "Then you'd never get any work done."

He grinned. "But I'd be a happier man."

Jokingly, she smacked his arm. "You'd get sick of me."

He shook his head, still smiling. "Nope. Not possible. You're stuck with me now."

He'd said it teasingly, but she hoped it were true. "I'm not interrupting anything, am I?"

"Are you kidding? How long can you stay?"

She bit her lip and wrapped her arms around his neck. "Until you kick me out."

He took her invitation and kissed her warmly. He nuzzled her as he pulled away, and then looked at her a little longer. "You seem different today. Is everything all right?"

"Yes. I'm great, actually. I just have some news."

When she paused to let the suspense rise, he laughed. "Out with it."

Suddenly, she was nervous about how he'd react. She brushed a speck of dust off his coat, unable to meet his eyes. "Well, I've been thinking a lot lately. About us."

Some of his humor vanished. "I hope there's *good* news at the end of this."

"There is. At least, I think there is." She looked him in the eye then. "I guess it depends on you."

He leaned back, taking her words seriously. "What is it?"

"I've been thinking about how things are progressing. I care about you. More than I thought I could."

His shoulders relaxed. "That's definitely a good thing."

"I want us to tell Rhys."

He froze, his eyes darting to hers again. "Are you sure?"

She could see he was trying to figure out what this meant. "I am. What do you think?"

"What do I think?" He looked at her like she was daft. "I should hope you know what I think." With a whoop, he picked her up and spun her in his arms around the cramped office. "I think this is incredible. Amazing. I'm so happy."

They both burst into laughter a moment before his head leaned down and his lips captured hers. They were caught up in the moment, in the joy of what this meant. Even though she hadn't told him she loved him—

And then the front door slammed shut.

She jerked away from Lucas, and he released her lips but kept his arm wrapped firmly around her. And when she turned toward the door, she was grateful he was holding her. "Rhys," she croaked, her knees buckling.

Her brother didn't speak, only watched the two of them, the muscle in his jaw ticking. He took a few deep breaths, calming himself before speaking. "I saw you ride into town and wanted to make sure you were all right. Looks like I needn't have worried." His voice was laced with sarcasm.

"Rhys, I can explain." She tried to step out of Lucas' arms, but he held her still.

Rhys raked a hand through his hair. "Explain what? Explain why you're kissing him? Explain why you're even with him? Abby, I thought you had more sense than this."

Her jaw dropped, but she wasn't outraged, she was hurt.

Lucas pulled her tightly against him. "Don't speak to her like that. I don't care if you're her brother or not. You're not going to treat her that way."

Rhys shook his head, bewildered. "When I told you to stay away from her unless she wanted you, I never thought in my wildest dreams that this would happen." His eyes turned to Abby. "Did he force you?"

"No! Of course not," she said, shocked her brother would even think such a thing.

Rhys nodded. "Then I have nothing else to say." He turned around and left, slamming the door behind him.

Abby flinched, and Lucas gave her a light squeeze. "He'll come around. It'll be all right."

"I don't know. I've never seen him so angry." She was worried.

"He's just surprised. Remember, he has no idea what's been happening."

She closed her eyes briefly and nodded. Lucas was right. They'd completely blindsided Rhys just now. She should have expected such a reaction. "I know. You're right. I just hate this." She let out a sound of distress and pulled away from him. "I'm sorry. I have to go after him, talk to him. I can't just leave it like this."

She glanced over her shoulder, and he nodded. "I understand. Let me come with you."

"No. This is something I have to do on my own. I think it'd only make it harder having you there."

"All right. If you're sure."

"I am."

He pulled her close and kissed her forehead, speaking into her hair. "Come back after you're done talking to him, so I know you're all right."

Her heart melted. This was exactly why she was in love with him. "I will." She brushed a kiss across his lips before releasing him and walking out the door.

It felt like a death march.

CHAPTER 16

Abby caught up to Rhys just as he entered the hotel. "Rhys, wait. Wait!" He didn't even slow.

She knew she looked ridiculous, chasing after her brother, yelling, but she didn't care. All she cared about was making this right, making him understand.

Rhys shook his head, waving her away, and she knew he was trying to control his temper, trying not to blow up. She normally appreciated that and gave him his space, but there was no avoiding it this time.

None of the employees stopped her as she followed him behind the desk to the *employees only* section of the hotel. "I'm going to follow you until you talk to me."

He glanced over his shoulder at her. "I suggest you don't do that. For your sake."

He continued on, but instead of listening to him, she notched her chin up and followed him into his office before closing the door.

"I'm warning you one last time. I'm not sure I can control my temper right now," he said. He moved behind his desk and sat down.

She shook her head. "We need to talk about this now, before it gets any worse."

He held up his hands. "I'm not sure what else there is to discuss. I think it was blatantly clear what's been happening."

"Fine, it's clear, but I still need to explain myself."

"Abby, you are your own woman. You don't need to explain anything to me."

She went to his desk and stood across from him, planting her hands and leaning forward. "I know I don't need to explain myself. But I want to. Rhys, I love you. You're my brother. You've always looked out for me. Always tried to protect me."

He scoffed. "And I thought I'd been doing a good job. But apparently, I'm a fool."

"You're not a fool." She lowered her head, unable to meet his eyes. "I was."

He grunted in obvious agreement, but it didn't deter her. "I'm a fool, but not for getting involved with Lucas again. I'm a fool for keeping it from you."

"Why did you? Why hide it?" Irritation tainted his voice.

She nodded slowly. "I deserve your anger. Not telling you what was happening was wrong. But I don't regret getting involved with him."

"How could you not? After what he did to you before, I thought you'd be smart enough to stay away."

"Well..." She tried to think of a way to explain it to him. "Could you stay away from Willow?"

His face turned hard. "That's not the same."

She cocked her head to the side "It is, actually. I know we were young, I know it was a long time ago, but Lucas and I truly loved each other back then. Over the years, I tried to convince myself that wasn't the case, that I couldn't have really loved him. But after he came here, I realized what I had felt for him had been true."

"Is that what this is then? Leftover feelings?"

She shook her head. "No. I was worried it was, at first, but no longer. I love him, Rhys." She let that statement linger in the air, remaining silent as her brother processed it.

Finally, he shook his head. "He left you once, Abby. How do you know he won't do that again? How do you know he's not involved with you just because he's here, because you're convenient?"

She suppressed a wince. What he said was valid, but it still hurt. "I know because I trust him. We talked about what happened before, about the decisions we made, and how our circumstances are different. Lucas has *changed*. Before, he was obsessed with success, with making something of himself. But now that he's accomplished it, he realizes that what he sacrificed to get there wasn't worth it."

Rhys rubbed the back of his neck. "I don't know, Abby. It's hard for a man to change, that I do know. Things are good right now, his business is doing well, but what happens if things go south? Will he abandon you again? Will he set off to reinvent himself?"

Rhys' words hit home, and a needle of doubt speared her, but she plucked it out. "I know that no matter what happens, he'll stick by my side."

"I hope so. For your sake, I truly hope so." He blew out a breath then met her eyes. "I can't bear to see you hurt again."

Love for her brother filled her heart. "Thank you for loving me as much as you do."

He let out a soft laugh. "It's a trial at times."

She grinned. "Don't I know it?" They both smiled at each other, the frustration on his face melting away. "Will you support me?" she finally asked.

"I don't like it, and I'm worried, but I'll always support you."

He stood up, and she moved around the desk, going into

his arms. She squeezed him tight before releasing him. "Thank you."

He nodded. "I just hope we don't come to regret this moment."

"Me either." She trusted Lucas, and she felt deep in her heart that everything would work out. She just needed to remember that.

✦

LUCAS NERVOUSLY PACED IN HIS OFFICE, FEELING AS IF every minute were an hour. He prayed Abby's conversation with her brother went well.

If it were only him, he wouldn't care what Rhys thought, but Abby did. And Abby would never be happy if she were estranged from her brother.

He swore and scrubbed a hand over his face. Maybe he should have insisted on telling Rhys up front, but he'd wanted Abby to feel comfortable, in control, and it was the only way she would agree to courting him.

What's done is done. They could only move forward, and he hoped Rhys would help them do that. But with how her brother had reacted, it could hurt Lucas' relationship with Abby. He couldn't bear if that happened. It'd taken everything in him to be patient, to wait and let her control the pace. He didn't know how much longer he could hold out.

When the door jingled, he spun toward it, ready to pounce on Abby. Instead, Connor stood in the doorway. "Good afternoon." He took his hat off in greeting.

Lucas widened his stance. "Is there something I can help you with?"

Connor spun his hat in his hands. "With mining?" He shook his head. "No. I have it handled. I came to talk to you about Abby."

122

"You came to talk to me about Abby?" Lucas asked the question slowly, trying to understand the man's audacity. "What more is there to say?"

Connor shrugged, confidently. "I just want to make sure there aren't any hard feelings between us."

"All right?"

Connor laughed. "I wanted you to know there aren't any hard feelings on my end."

Since Abby had just told him she wanted to tell Rhys about their relationship, Lucas found it highly unlikely Connor was aware of it. "Why would you have any hard feelings?"

"Because you tried to steal Abby from me."

"Steal Abby...from you?" Even more confusion filled him. "I'm sorry, I have no idea what you're talking about."

Connor's chin notched up. "I've asked Abby to marry me."

Relief filled Lucas. Obviously, there was a misunderstanding. "I'm sorry you were disappointed."

"Who said I was disappointed?"

Lucas frowned. "Abby is with me."

"That's not the impression she gave me." Connor shook his head regretfully, like he pitied Lucas.

Doubt wormed its way into Lucas' heart. "When did you ask her to marry you?"

"The night I drove her home after the job fair."

"And she didn't turn you down?"

Connor shook his head slowly. "No. She said she'd consider it."

That made a little more sense. "I'm sorry to tell you, but I think she's made up her mind and just hasn't had an opportunity to refuse you."

Connor rocked back on his heels. "I've seen her a few times since then. There was plenty of time for her to let me down. Last I heard, she was still thinking about it."

Lucas didn't know what was happening right now. If what Connor said was true, and he assumed it was, then what was Abby thinking? She'd told him she wanted to tell Rhys about their relationship, signaling her desire to be with him—but then she hadn't rejected Connor? None of it made sense.

Lucas shook his head. "I'm sorry, I don't know what was said between the two of you, but there must be some misunderstanding."

Connor just looked at Lucas was sympathy. "She does that to a man, doesn't she? She's so sweet and quiet, she's in a man's heart before he even realizes it."

Lucas snorted. "I'm sorry, are we talking about Abigail Winthrop?"

Connor's eyebrows lowered as if Lucas had insulted her. "Who else would we be speaking of?"

"I wasn't sure. Because the woman you just described is nothing like Abby."

Irritation crossed Connor's face. "Maybe you don't know Abby as well as you think you do."

Lucas didn't know what to think at this point. Connor didn't appear to be going away, and Lucas couldn't talk any sense into the man. "I guess we're not going to be able to resolve this until Abby returns."

"Fine with me." Connor placed his hat on his head. "Doesn't matter to me how you come around to the truth, but I thought it was right to inform you of my relationship with Abby and how serious it is."

The urge to tell Connor exactly his relationship with Abby was overwhelming, but he choked it back. This wasn't a competition. All that mattered was what Abby truly felt.

He wanted to think she was in love with him, but she hadn't said that, had she? He thought over their conversation earlier, and he realized she'd only said she wanted to tell Rhys about their relationship.

Dread settled in his gut. Was it possible she didn't feel as strongly as he thought? She must be considering a future with him if she wanted to tell Rhys. But then again, maybe she was tired of lying to her brother? Maybe she just wanted to set the record straight.

And if that were true, maybe she *was* considering marrying Connor.

An ache settled through him. He wanted to rage, to growl like a wounded animal, but he held it in.

Right as he was about to tell Connor to leave, the bell above the door chimed again, and Abby walked in, a grin on her face as she stepped in the door.

That smile slowly left as she looked between Lucas and Connor and closed the door behind her.

Connor tipped his hat with a grin. "Good afternoon, Abby. I'm happy to see you."

"Connor. What are you doing here?" She seemed bewildered and darted a worried glance at Lucas.

His heart froze as he saw the truth on her face. What Connor said was true. He'd proposed to her, and she still hadn't turned him down. *Is she playing me false?* He would've never thought such a thing possible, but then again, Abby had changed. His spine stiffened.

Connor stepped forward, taking her hand, and Abby allowed it. Lucas wanted to howl, but instead, he held himself rigid. If Abby wanted this man to hold her hand, to marry her, Lucas would let her. He meant it when he said it was her choice, and no matter what happened, no matter how much it destroyed him, he wouldn't stand in her way.

Connor cleared his throat. "I was hoping to see you. I also thought it right for Mr. McDermott to know that I asked for your hand in marriage."

Abby's wide eyes darted back to Lucas.

Even though he knew the truth, he still needed to hear her say it. "Is it true? That Connor asked you to marry him and you haven't said no?" He stood in place, refusing to go to her.

She chewed her lip. "It is. I was going to tell you."

He held up his hand. "You don't need to tell me anything. As I said before, this is your choice."

"Lucas, it's not like that."

He wanted to hear her explanation, hoping it would ease the hurt inside, but he refused to have that talk in front of Connor, who still stood between them, a satisfied grin on his face. Lucas knew it wasn't the man's intention to tear him down, just to stake his claim on Abby. And he obviously felt as though he'd been successful.

Connor lowered his head apologetically. "I'm sorry this has made you uncomfortable, Abby. Why don't I take you home?"

Lucas' jaw locked. He wanted to tell Connor to get out and to force Abby to tell him what she truly wanted. But instead, he remained quiet. It was her choice.

"We can talk about this later, if you want," he said, seeing her struggling.

Her shoulders fell. "Lucas..." But she didn't say anything else. What else could she say?

"It's all right. I understand."

"I meant everything I said earlier." Her eyes pleaded, she wanted him to understand that this wasn't the time to explain it. If only Connor would leave.

He nodded. And finally, as if realizing she wouldn't be able to set this right, she turned to Connor and smiled, taking his offered arm.

After Connor escorted her out, Lucas stood still for several minutes, counting his breaths, attempting to control his emotions. This had to be some sort of misunderstanding. He knew Abby. No matter how much time had passed, she would never deceive him like this. If she said she wanted to tell Rhys about them, it's because she wanted to be with him. He had to believe that.

Accepting his conclusion, he nodded to himself. This would all work out. He just had to remain patient. He was meant to be with Abby.

Reassured, he went back to his work, putting the entire situation out of his mind as he worked through one problem with the mine after another. An hour had gone by when a knock sounded on the door.

He'd closed up for the day, not being in the mood to interact with others, so he ignored it. But when the knock came again, he cursed, and rose from his chair.

He looked out the front window and opened the door quickly when he saw the Western Union agent. "Do you have something for me?"

The man nodded. "Yes, sir." Without further delay, he handed Lucas a telegram.

Lucas opened it, scanning the brief message before cursing. "This just came in?"

"Yes, sir."

There was trouble with the bank in St. Louis, and they needed Lucas immediately. He tried to come up with a way to speak with Abby before leaving on the next train in an hour, but it would be impossible. He'd seen her ride out of town alone, and assumed she'd returned home.

He scrubbed a hand over his face. What a mess.

"Will you answer, sir?"

He nodded grimly. "Tell Eversly, I'm on my way."

"Very good, sir." The man left quickly to deliver his message.

Lucas quickly cleaned up his desk, barely having enough

time to pack before rushing to the train. But he couldn't leave Abby without telling her where he'd gone and reassuring her they would finish their discussion when he got back. It gutted him to leave before resolving this, but the problem in St. Louis couldn't wait. His partners were depending on him.

He grabbed a fresh sheet of paper at the ticketing counter and scribbled a quick note, apologizing profusely, and telling her how much she meant to him.

He just hoped it was enough.

CHAPTER 17

The next day, Abby rode into town, anxious to speak with Lucas. When she'd left his office with Connor yesterday, she knew Lucas wasn't happy, but she was grateful he'd behaved how he had. He'd allowed her to make the choice and hadn't forced his will upon her or demanded she explain herself.

If she had any doubts before, his behavior had erased them. Lucas was the man she wanted to be with, and no matter what, today she was going to tell him she loved him.

Connor had been disappointed when she'd told him she was in love with someone else. Obviously, it hadn't been the answer he wanted, but after his initial upset, he'd kissed her hand and told her he hoped she found happiness.

She was determined to do just that.

She dismounted in front of Lucas' office, her heart light now that she didn't have to sneak around to see him. They were free to be with each other, and nothing had ever felt so good.

She quickly walked up the boardwalk to the door, placed

her hand on the knob, and pushed. But the door wouldn't open. She tried again, frowning—it was locked.

She looked through the window but couldn't see Lucas. Was he still at the hotel?

She looked again to confirm he wasn't there before mounting her horse and riding to the hotel. She hoped he wasn't ill.

She smiled gratefully when her brother's employees took care of her horse. She entered the hotel, feeling confident. She'd see Lucas in a few moments, and the uneasiness in her heart would vanish.

The clerk at the desk greeted her. "Is there something I can help you with, Miss Winthrop? Are you here to see Mr. Winthrop?"

"No. Thank you. I'm here to see Mr. McDermott. Have you seen him?"

The clerk's brows furrowed. "I'm sorry, but Mr. McDermott checked out yesterday."

She froze. "No. That's not possible. I know he's staying here longer."

"I'm sorry." Double checking the ledger, the clerk shook his head again. "No. He checked out before the last train left. I overheard him saying he was heading to St. Louis."

Her stomach dropped. That couldn't be true. "Are you absolutely certain?"

He nodded regretfully. "I am. I'm sorry."

Tears sprang to her eyes, but she shook her head, forcing them back. "No. It's all right."

He looked concerned. "May I...may I get Mr. Winthrop?"

She dashed her tears and shook her head even more forcefully. Seeing Rhys was the last thing she wanted. He'd warned her about this, warned her not to get involved again with Lucas, but she'd done just that. She'd been every inch as stupid as he thought she was. "No. I'm perfectly all right. Thank you."

Blindly, she whirled around, walking toward the exit.

"Abby?" The voice sounded far away. "Abby?"

Just as she was about to step to the door, a delicate finger tapped her shoulder, and she looked over at Lily.

Lily wrapped her arm around Abby's shoulders, and ushered her out of the lobby. Fresh air filled her lungs. "I have the wagon. I'll take you home."

"No. My horse—"

"They'll board it at the hotel."

She didn't have the will to argue. Numbness wove through her, starting from her toes and working up slowly toward her heart.

"Just tell me, are you injured?" Lily said quietly.

Abby wasn't certain how to answer that. Physically, she was fine. But inside, she felt as though a knife had separated her heart in two. "I have no injuries. At least, nothing you can see."

Without another word, Lily helped her into the wagon and went around to drive. Mere moments later, they made their way outside town.

And as they passed the last house, it was like the dam on her emotions burst. She sobbed, her face falling into her hands as big, thick tears splattered onto her skirt. She sucked in heaving breaths, but only felt as though she would be sick. She gasped, her lungs closing, refusing to let air in.

"Just keep breathing. In and out," Lily said. "You're going to be fine. Whatever happened, it's going to be all right."

Abby closed her eyes tight, shaking her head, denying Lily's words. Nothing would ever be all right again. "He left. Lucas left without a word," she said, barely able to get the words out.

Lily gasped. "Why? What happened?"

"After the hiring fair, Connor Broderick asked me to marry him, and I didn't immediately reject him. I wasn't sure how things would work out with Lucas, and I wanted to give Connor the respect he deserved by thinking it over. But yesterday, Connor told Lucas about the proposal, so I left with Connor to break it off and was so exhausted from it all, I didn't return to Lucas. I thought it would be fine to talk to him today after we'd both rested. Apparently, he left on the train yesterday afternoon."

Lily blew out a long breath. "I'm so sorry this happened. Perhaps you can send him a letter and explain? It sounds like a misunderstanding."

Abby wished it were so easy that a letter would solve everything. But a letter wouldn't fix what had happened. Lucas had *left* her. It didn't matter what the reason was. He left without saying a word, just like he had all those years ago. She thought he'd changed, but *nothing* had changed. Nothing ever would.

She sobbed again, and Lily brought her arm around her, pulling her in tight. "It's going to be all right. We'll figure out a way."

When Abby couldn't stop the tears, couldn't speak through the sobs, Lily just held her. It was the greatest kindness anyone had ever done for her.

Finally, as they rounded the last corner to home and Ivan's house came into view, she realized her time here was finished. Her gasps for air subsided, her tears slowed, and she sucked in a deep breath, letting it out shakily. "I can't stay here anymore."

"What? Why?"

"I've lived here for over a year, and I've loved every moment of it. This place brought me peace and independence and a fresh start. But none of that is possible anymore. The Copper Kings, *Lucas*, has rented it. He might be gone, but he'll be back to do his job. His business is here, the mine is here, and no matter what happened between us, he still needs to return to this house to help you all. I can't bear to see him again. It hurts too much. I—I'm not strong enough." She lowered her head, ashamed.

Lily bit her lip, and tears filled her big blue eyes. "It won't be the same without you. You're one of us."

Abby took her hand. "Me moving doesn't change that. You'll be moving out soon too. All of you will. I'm just sorry it had to happen this way."

Lily nodded and squeezed her hand. "I understand. But where will you go?"

"The hotel, for now. But soon I'll buy my own house." She looked up at the mansion, silently saying goodbye. "This one was never mine. I was just a visitor, but I love Promise Creek. I'm never leaving." She sniffled and sat up straighter. "Besides, I have the money to buy any home I desire. And that's exactly what I'll do."

"Do you want me to tell the others?"

"No. I'll do it. They should hear from me."

"I'll be right beside you."

"I'd like that. I'm lucky to have you as a friend."

Lily gently bumped shoulders with her. "Now and forever."

And in that moment, Abby realized she'd gotten what she'd wanted most of all. A sisterhood. No matter where she went, no matter where *they* went, they would always have each other.

A WEEK LATER, LUCAS GOT OFF THE MIDDAY TRAIN TO Promise Creek, exhausted, hungry, and weary from traveling. But all of that could wait until after he saw Abby. Leaving the way he had, unable to see her, had been torture. She had to feel the same, but he hoped the letter the train station had delivered would reassure her of his feelings and intentions toward her.

He signaled the porter, giving him his luggage ticket and instructions to deliver his trunk to the hotel.

Luckily, Rhys kept horses available at the hotel for guests, so that would save him some time. He didn't want to spend any more time away from Abby than necessary.

He'd still give her the time she needed to decide, but he wanted to make sure she knew he loved her. He'd been stupid not to tell her that from the moment he realized it—he just hadn't wanted to push her. But surely telling her his feelings wasn't forcing her hand. He'd make her realize he didn't expect anything in return. He just wanted to give her everything.

He walked into the hotel, and a sense of homecoming washed over him. They wouldn't continue to live in the hotel after they were married, but he realized and felt what Abby loved about Promise Creek. There was something about it, something that called to him. They'd have to travel for work on occasion, but if Abby wanted to, he'd be more than happy to settle here.

A grin filled his face just thinking of all the things he wanted to tell her. With any luck, he'd convince her to marry him this week.

He stepped up to the desk and nodded to the clerk before requesting another room.

The boy shuffled uneasily. "I'm sorry, Mr. McDermott, but we are unable to offer you a room at this time."

The smile faltered on Lucas' face. "I beg your pardon?"

The clerk swallowed thickly. "Mr. Winthrop has informed us that you are no longer welcome here."

"Is that so?"

Realizing it was better to remain silent, the clerk nodded.

Before Lucas could say anything further, a voice interrupted their conversation. "I'll handle this."

Lucas turned slowly, facing an angry Rhys. "You changed your mind then?" Lucas asked. "You're making choices for Abby now?"

Rhys smiled, but there was nothing kind in his expression. "No. *You* changed her mind. All on your own."

"What are you talking about?"

Rhys shrugged. "You left her. Just like I told her you would. Finally, she realized I was right. She'll never be happy with you."

"It was an emergency. I had to go. There was no time to talk to her about it. I explained it all in my note. Didn't she get it?"

"All I know is that she's done with you. That makes me done with you as well."

Panic ignited in his gut. "I have to see her. Now."

Lucas spun on his heel, but before he could take more than three steps, Rhys stopped him. "Where are you going?"

"To the house. This is all a misunderstanding."

"You left. Where's the misunderstanding in that?"

That was the last straw. Lucas wheeled around, grabbing Rhys by the coat. "I didn't leave her. I'll *never* leave her. I love her more than the air I breathe. And if you think to stand in my way, think again. *Nothing* will stop me from going to Abby; nothing will stop me from telling her how I feel. And if she doesn't want me, nothing will stop me from spending the rest of my life trying to win her back."

Instead of flicking him off, Rhys cocked his head and

considered Lucas. Finally, he nodded. "You truly mean that, don't you?"

"Do you think this is some sort of game?" Disgusted, Lucas released him.

Rhys smoothed his coat. "No. But I thought *you* did. I thought you didn't care about her, that it wouldn't matter to you if she was hurt."

Rage flowed through him. "I would rather gut myself than cause her one moment of hurt."

"You really left her a letter?"

"Yes. I asked the train station to deliver it." His gut clenched. "She didn't receive it?" Rhys shook his head, and Lucas swore, imagining what she must think.

Fear shot through him. Would she forgive him? Or had he lost her forever? How could he convince her to trust him?

Rhys let out a long breath. "I can't believe I'm saying this, but I believe you. Look, Abby loves you. It's obvious, and I can also see you love her. All I want—all that I've ever wanted —is her happiness."

Lucas met his eyes. "That's all I want for her as well. Even if it's not with me."

Understanding passed between them, and Rhys nodded. "She's in the library."

"Pardon?"

Rhys nodded toward the employee hallway. "She's in the library."

Lucas hesitated. "Why are you helping me?"

"Even though I don't like what happened, you're who she wants. And after having her here this week, I don't think this is something she'll move on from."

"Thank you."

Rhys nodded once. "Make her happy. And if you screw this up, I'll destroy you."

Lucas felt the first glimmer of a smile. Most people would

think Rhys' threat an empty one, but Lucas knew it was fact. "I'll make her happy."

Rhys just waved him on. "I'll be in the dining room with my wife if you need anything."

All Lucas needed was Abby.

CHAPTER 18

Abby tried reading the same page three times before closing the book with a snap. It'd been a week since Lucas left, and the pain of it was still fresh. She was like the living dead, walking from her room to the library and back, refusing to go into the public areas. The library was usually open to guests, but Rhys had closed it during her stay.

She didn't know what she'd do without her brother.

She stood and replaced the book on the shelf, idly gazing over the spines of the books next to it, but she couldn't bring herself to pick one. In truth, she didn't care what she read, she didn't care where she was, and she didn't care what she did.

Life had no meaning. She'd felt similarly when Lucas had left her years ago, but she'd been so young, and there had been plenty to occupy her time with, things to fill the void. It had helped to have a semblance of a life, and eventually, she'd rejoined the living. But this was different.

Back then, she'd had hope she would meet someone else. That she would marry. But she now knew it would never happen. Lucas was it for her. Her one great love. And having him leave her again had not only broken her heart, it had destroyed it.

She heard the door open behind her, and she shook her head. "I mean it, Rhys. I'm not going to the dining room. I need a few more days."

The door closed softly, and she was grateful her brother had listened to her.

"I bet we could get the chef to make you your favorite."

She gasped and spun around, her hand flying to her heart. "Lucas! What are you doing here?" Her eyes ran over him, greedy to see him. He was disheveled, his hair standing on end in different directions, his suit wrinkled like he'd slept in it. "Did you just come in on the train?"

He leaned against the door and slowly crossed his arms and ankles. "I did. I traveled through the night to get here."

His words hurt. He probably had more work to do. She didn't want him to see her face, so she turned back toward the shelf, pretending to organize the books. "I see. Well, whatever you came back for must be important. I won't keep you." She was grateful her voice sounded even, when everything inside her was chaos.

His footfalls sounded as he crossed the room to stand behind her, but he didn't touch her. "What I came back for *is* important. More important than anything else in my life."

She squeezed her eyes shut, knowing he spoke the truth. Business—success—would always come first to him. "Good. Then you should leave and tend to it."

"Don't you want to ask what it is?" When she didn't immediately respond, he said, "Look at me."

She wanted to deny him, to tell him no, to scream for him to get out, but she didn't do any of those things. She turned toward him, the unshed tears in her eyes brimming until he looked like a wet blur. "What more do you want from me? What more can I give?"

His arms fell to his sides. "Abby—" his words strangled at the end.

She laughed mirthlessly. "What? Did you expect me to be all right? You left me, Lucas. *You left*."

He nodded, accepting everything she said. "I did. I received an urgent message and had to leave immediately. If I hadn't, things would've fallen apart. And while I would've allowed it to happen if it were just me, I have a responsibility to my partners. I couldn't abandon them."

She held up her hand. "I understand. I understand what comes first to you, and I don't even blame you. I can't change who you are. I can't change what you want. All I can give is me. Nothing else."

"That's all I want."

She shook her head, denying his words. "Don't. Don't say that. You don't mean it."

"I do. I love you, Abby. I love you so much it hurts. I loved you then and now and for all the time in between. You have always been in my heart, the woman I was meant to be with. I've made mistakes, there's no denying that, but I'm not making a mistake now. I *love* you. I never meant to leave you, and if you believe anything, believe that. There wasn't enough time to see you before I had to leave. But I wrote you a letter and asked the train station to deliver it."

She jerked her head away. "There was no letter."

Gently, he placed his hand on the side of her face and brought her gaze to his. "I did write you a letter. And in it I told you that I love you, that I would hate being away from you, and that I would come back as soon as I could to be by your side."

Fresh tears filled her eyes. She wanted to believe him, yearned to, but she was afraid. "I didn't get it."

His face was serious as he nodded. "I know. More than

anything, I hate that you're hurt. I'll find out what happened to the letter, but know that I did write it. That I love you. I never meant to leave you. I want to spend the rest of my life with you."

Tears trailed down her face, and he brought his other hand up, using his thumbs to wipe the moisture away. "Abby, please." He looked tortured by her tears, and she realized then that he truly meant everything he'd said.

Her heart opened, letting him in, letting in every single thing he'd said. "I love you."

Relief crossed his face a second before his mouth took hers. The kiss was raw and honest and everything she'd ever hoped for. He pulled away after a moment, his breath sawing in and out of his lungs. His hand still held her face as he searched her eyes. "You mean it, don't you?"

She smiled at the uncertainty in his voice, the fear, and placed one of her hands over his, squeezing. "I do. I love you, Lucas. I always have. But when I thought you left again, it destroyed me. I didn't know how I'd go on."

"I'll never leave you. I'll always be here. I love you so much that I hate being away from you for even a moment."

"I do too."

He let out a breath of relief and brought his forehead to hers. "Then marry me." He leaned back and looked into her eyes, his gaze pleading with her. "Marry me today, tomorrow, this week. Please. Just say you'll be my wife, because I never want to be without you again."

Her chin wobbled, but she smiled as more tears trailed down her cheeks. "Yes. Yes, I'll marry you." A laugh escaped her lips.

Relief filled his face, and he brought her lips to his, sealing her words, filling her heart.

That morning had seemed so bleak she hadn't known how she'd live through the rest of her life. But now the world was beautiful once again. She was happy, and she had the love of her life by her side.

Years without Lucas had taught her how to survive, but for the first time, she felt as though she were truly living. And she couldn't wait to live every day, every moment, with the man she loved.

EPILOGUE

A bby paused in the doorway of her husband's home office, leaning against the frame, and watched him. *My husband*, she thought. It never got old thinking of Lucas that way. He was hunched over his desk, scribbling some notes. His shirtsleeves were rolled up, the top two buttons of his shirt undone.

It was a sight she often saw now that they'd moved into the home he'd had built for her. She was grateful to be so close to town, to Rhys and Willow, and it was big enough to fit any number of children.

After four years of marriage, they continued to fall even more in love. And with how impossible it was to keep their hands off each other, more children were inevitable.

She chuckled to herself, and the sound drew his attention. Immediately, he smiled and leaned back in his chair. "Come here."

She didn't even hesitate at the warm look in his eyes. When she got to him, he scooted back from the desk and pulled her across his lap, cradling her in his arms. "What were you laughing at?"

Grinning, she wrapped her arms around him. "About how much I still want you after all this time."

He leaned in, kissing her neck, before whispering, "I'll never have enough of you."

Pleasure filled her at his words. "I'll never have enough of you either," she said softly.

He tilted her head toward him and kissed her softly, deeply, setting her body on fire. She'd thought that as time passed the way she felt about him, her desire, would fade. But it had only gotten stronger. She whimpered when he stopped. "I wish bedtime wasn't so far away."

His smile came on slowly, wickedly. "Who said we had to wait for bed?"

"I wasn't talking about *our* bedtime." She rolled her eyes playfully.

His brow lifted, and a squeal sounded at the doorway. "Daddy!" Their two-year-old son exclaimed, toddling into the room.

Abby and Lucas burst into giggles at their son's antics.

"Oh, he's seen you now," Abby said between chuckles. "It looks as though your work is done for the evening."

Lucas snorted, his eyes gazing adoringly at his son. "And I don't mind." When Atticus was close enough, Lucas scooped him up and placed him on Abby's lap so he could hold them both snuggled in his arms. "How did I get so lucky?"

Abby turned her head, kissing him tenderly. "I ask myself the same thing every day. Thank you for giving us such a wonderful life."

He shook his head, and she looked at him curiously. "You're the one who has given me everything." His eyes wandered to their son and then back to her. "Without you, life isn't worth living."

Her heart clenched. "I love you."

"I love you too." He leaned forward a few inches so his

lips brushed her hair. "I think bedtime should come early tonight."

He leaned back, and she looked at him, her eyes twinkling. "I think so too."

Their son let out another squeal, trying to climb her to get to Lucas. She laughed and rolled her eyes before standing.

Lucas rose, cradling his son, and brushed a kiss across his forehead as he listened intently to Atticus' jabbering. But before Abby made her way out the door, he took her hand and brought it to his lips. They left the room, holding hands.

No more work happened that night. Instead, the candles dimmed as they showed each other how much they were loved, needed, and wanted. Life was even more wonderful than Abby had ever imagined. With Lucas by her side, all things were possible.

*****

Thank you for reading Western Bride! I hope you loved Abby & Lucas' story. If you did, please consider leaving a review. Reviews help other readers find books they might like, and I'd appreciate it so much!

If you haven't already, sign up for my newsletter at www.-janelledaniels.com! The next Copper King will be out shortly, and you won't want to miss it! <3
-Janelle Daniels

FREE DOWNLOAD

**Will Father Christmas bring
them their happily ever after?**

★★★★★ 4.3 out of 5 stars

Get your free copy of A Christmas
Secret when you opt-in to the
Janelle Daniels Readers Club.
Get started here:

http://www.janelledaniels.com/claim-your-free-book.html

TITLES BY JANELLE DANIELS

Copper Kings

Western Bride (Copper Kings – Book 1)

Miners to Millionaires

A Mail-Order Heart (Miners to Millionaires – Book 1)

A Mail-Order Wish (Miners to Millionaires – Book 2)

A Mail-Order Hope (Miners to Millionaires – Book 3)

A Mail-Order Dream (Miners to Millionaires – Book 4)

A Mail-Order Chance (Miners to Millionaires – Book 5)

A Mail-Order Dawn (Miners to Millionaires – Book 6)

A Mail-Order Escape (Miners to Millionaires – Book 7)

A Mail-Order Illusion (Miners to Millionaires – Book 8)

A Mail-Order Haven (Miners to Millionaires – Book 9)

A Mail-Order Destiny (Miners to Millionaires – Book 10)

Scandals & Secrets

Scandal of Love (Scandals & Secrets – Book 1)

Masquerade Secrets (Scandals & Secrets – Book 2)

Secrets in Mourning (Scandals & Secrets – Book 3)

A Kiss with Scandal (Scandals & Secrets – Book 4)

A Christmas Secret (Scandals & Secrets – Book 4.5)

Single Title Romance

Sunkissed

My Only Wish

Collaborations

Kitty: Bride of Hawaii (American Mail-Order Brides)

Falling for a Duke (Timeless Regency Collection)

The Witches of Redwood Falls

The Witching Moon (The Witches of Redwood Falls – Book 1)

The Witches Craft (The Witches of Redwood Falls – Book 2)

WESTERN BRIDE

Dream Cache Publishing

This is a work of fiction. Names, characters, places, and incidents either are products of the author's imagination or are used fictitiously. Any resemblance to actual events or locales or persons, living or dead, is entirely coincidental.

www.janelledaniels.com

Copyright © 2018 by Janelle Daniels

Cover Art © 2018 Erin Dameron-Hill

All rights reserved.